RWBY

FAIRY TALES OF

REMNANT

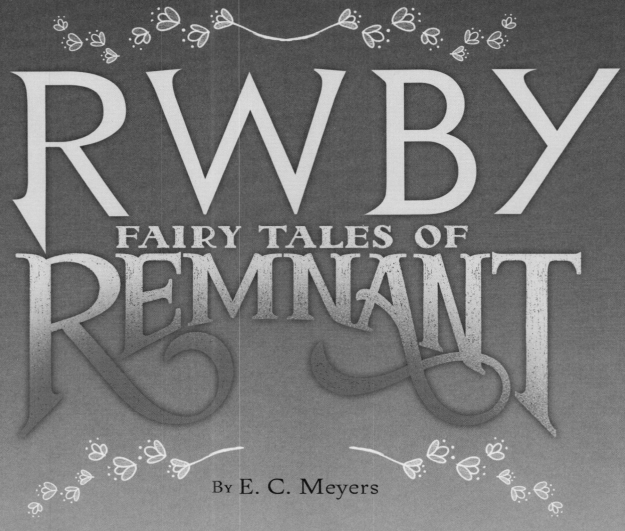

RWBY
FAIRY TALES OF
REMNANT

By E. C. Meyers

ILLUSTRATED BY Violet Tobacco

BASED ON THE SERIES CREATED BY Monty Oum

 Scholastic Inc.
New York

ROOSTER TEETH®

© 2020 Rooster Teeth Productions, LLC

Cover texture photo © aga7ta/Shutterstock.

ISBN 978-1-338-65208-6

10 9 8 7 6 5 4 3 2 1   20 21 22 23 24

Printed in China   38

First printing 2020

Book design by Betsy Peterschmidt • Illustrations by Violet Tobacco

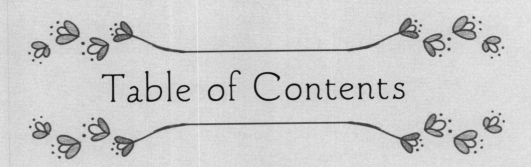

Table of Contents

Introduction

Remnant has a very long history, and yet we do not know much about its ancient past. We have many questions, and never all the answers we would like. But we do have stories. Whether they're true stories passed down through the ages or myths defying time itself, our stories help explain who we are and why we're here They give us solace when we need it, advice if we seek it, and connections that bind us together as one people. If you don't believe in stories, if you can't accept their truths, then you will always seek and never find.

When I became headmaster of Beacon Academy, one of my first goals was to introduce a deeper study

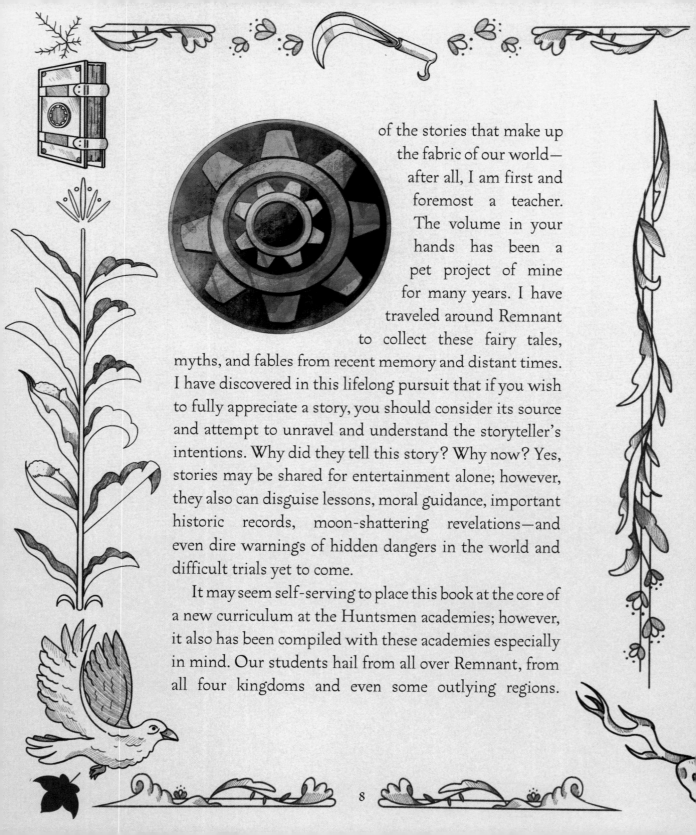

of the stories that make up the fabric of our world—after all, I am first and foremost a teacher. The volume in your hands has been a pet project of mine for many years. I have traveled around Remnant to collect these fairy tales, myths, and fables from recent memory and distant times. I have discovered in this lifelong pursuit that if you wish to fully appreciate a story, you should consider its source and attempt to unravel and understand the storyteller's intentions. Why did they tell this story? Why now? Yes, stories may be shared for entertainment alone; however, they also can disguise lessons, moral guidance, important historic records, moon-shattering revelations—and even dire warnings of hidden dangers in the world and difficult trials yet to come.

It may seem self-serving to place this book at the core of a new curriculum at the Huntsmen academies; however, it also has been compiled with these academies especially in mind. Our students hail from all over Remnant, from all four kingdoms and even some outlying regions.

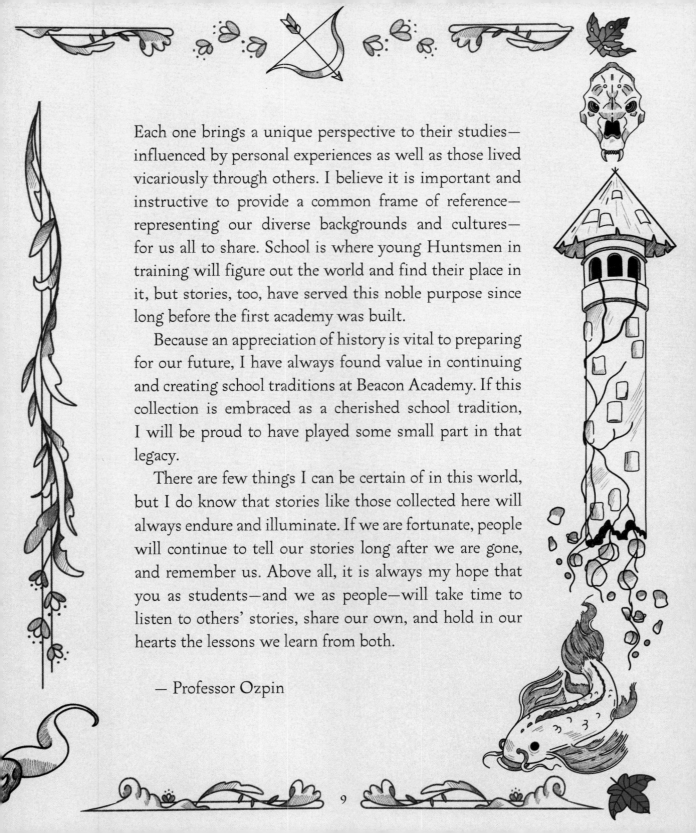

Each one brings a unique perspective to their studies—influenced by personal experiences as well as those lived vicariously through others. I believe it is important and instructive to provide a common frame of reference—representing our diverse backgrounds and cultures—for us all to share. School is where young Huntsmen in training will figure out the world and find their place in it, but stories, too, have served this noble purpose since long before the first academy was built.

Because an appreciation of history is vital to preparing for our future, I have always found value in continuing and creating school traditions at Beacon Academy. If this collection is embraced as a cherished school tradition, I will be proud to have played some small part in that legacy.

There are few things I can be certain of in this world, but I do know that stories like those collected here will always endure and illuminate. If we are fortunate, people will continue to tell our stories long after we are gone, and remember us. Above all, it is always my hope that you as students—and we as people—will take time to listen to others' stories, share our own, and hold in our hearts the lessons we learn from both.

— Professor Ozpin

The Warrior in the Woods

As recorded by Glynda Goodwitch

There was once a village on the edge of a lush forest, known far and wide as the safest place in the land. The evil creatures of Grimm had not attacked there since long before anyone could remember, and it was said that the woods themselves protected the people from harm: as long as no one dared to enter the charmed forest, it would keep the monsters at bay.

The people went about their days with carefree spirits, and the village gradually grew as more people arrived to live in peace. Over time, the people grew complacent in their ways, taking their fortune for granted and trusting they would always be safe and happy. The village children began playing games inside the woods, though they never ventured too far. After all, they'd never even seen a Grimm outside a storybook.

One day, a boy was playing hide and seek with his friends in the woods. He ventured farther inside than ever before, farther than anyone would ever think to look for him. He waited and waited, alone in the gloomy forest. As night fell, the boy heard the woods come alive with the sounds of flapping wings, skittering insects, and rustling leaves. But he had never been afraid of the dark before, and he had always been curious about the forest, so instead of returning home to a hot meal and a warm fire, he wandered deeper into the trees.

The boy soon found his way into a moonlit clearing, and there something found him. He first saw its four glowing red eyes, then the stark white of its long, sharp, curved tusks. This was the largest creature the boy had ever seen, and its pitch-black hair was seemingly made of the night itself.

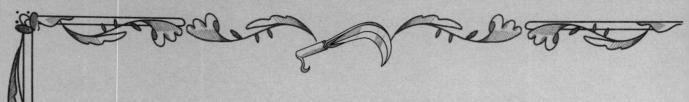

He screamed! The boy couldn't help it, for he had never seen anything like the Grimm. For the first time in his life, he knew fear, and he felt sure he was about to die.

The creature whirled on him, fixed the boy in its burning gaze, and charged. The boy froze, throwing his arms up in front of him and squeezing his eyes shut. But then, as he braced for the worst, something shoved him aside. He tumbled away, through loose dirt, stones, and leaves. And when he looked up he saw a tall, fair woman in a flowing black cape facing off against the Grimm. She gripped a long-handled billhook with both hands.

The boy was stunned to see the boar-like Grimm turn to run away from her. The woman charged after it, her bladed staff spinning so fast that it blurred.

Just before she caught up to the Grimm, the woman planted the butt end of the weapon into the earth and vaulted feet-first into the air. As she soared over the creature, she turned in midair, sweeping the hooked blade down and slicing through the Grimm. It squealed and split in two. When the woman landed, she pivoted to face the Grimm again, but the broken pieces only puffed into thick black smoke and floated away. She spun the billhook once more and holstered it on her back.

"Go home. You never saw me," she told the boy, turning to leave.

The boy jumped up. "Wait!" he said. His ankle was sprained, but he hobbled after the woman, grimacing. She paused and looked back, and that was the first time he truly saw her. She was as beautiful as she was fierce.

Up close, he saw her black cloak was threadbare, its hem tattered, tears throughout it mended with fraying red thread. Her loose gray blouse might have been white once, and her leggings were covered in mismatched patches. Her hair was almost as dark as the Grimm's, white hairs standing out as brightly as bone. The metal hook on her weapon was chipped and a crack was beginning to split the long wooden handle.

"Thank you," he said simply.

She nodded and continued to move away.

"At least tell me your name!" he called after her. But she disappeared into the trees.

The boy limped home. He didn't tell anyone about the warrior woman who had saved him, but he described the terrible monster he had narrowly escaped. Those who believed him took his safe return as proof that the woods protected them, and they continued living as they had. But the boy had seen the truth, so he watched the woods with

caution, always remembering the woman. And he wondered: who was she, and why had she saved him? Was it she that kept the whole village safe?

A year later, the boy returned to the clearing in the woods, and then he dared to go beyond it. Even during the day it was dark amid the trees, and after some time he realized he was being followed. A sense of dread overcame him, and when he looked over his shoulder, he saw two bright yellow eyes flaring in the shadows. He drew a dagger from his belt and only faltered when the creature crashed through the trees and howled before him.

This Grimm had a gruesome, bony mask and it was sharp all over: sharp teeth, sharp spikes, sharp claws. It bounded toward him on four massive paws, its hind legs built for speed and power. The boy raised his dagger, but it was almost as useless as if he had been unarmed. He didn't cry out or try to run away—he was frozen in place by fear.

Just then, he saw the woman drop from a tree onto the creature's back and hack at its neck with her billhook. Its handle was shorter now, and the boy saw she carried a sharpened stake made from its other, broken half.

When the Grimm tried to shake her off,

she jammed the stake into one of its eyes. Then she jumped off and watched as the terrible, dark wolf toppled backward and dissolved into a cloud of mist. She retrieved the stake, its tip steaming.

"Thank you," the boy said, finding his voice. She turned to him.

"You again?" She shook her head and walked off.

The boy felt an unexpected rush of joy. "You remember me?"

"I remember everyone I've saved. And everyone I didn't." She paused to look at him. "I see you didn't learn your lesson about coming into my woods."

He held up the dagger. "I came prepared."

Her laugh was not unkind. "So you're a slow learner. Don't come back. Really."

"I came looking for you," he admitted.

She narrowed her eyes. "I don't train people to fight anymore."

"It's not that. I brought you something." The boy pulled off his backpack and held it out to her. She hesitated before coming closer to take it. She wasn't as tall as she had seemed before, and there were more white strands in her hair. But she was still proud and strong, and even more beautiful than he remembered.

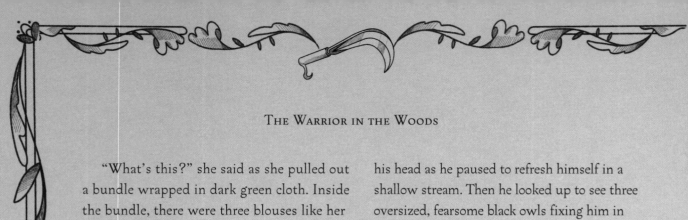

"What's this?" she said as she pulled out a bundle wrapped in dark green cloth. Inside the bundle, there were three blouses like her own, two leggings, a black skirt, new boots, and a short, hooded green cloak.

"New clothes," he said. "Well, not new really. They were my mother's."

Her brief smile faded. "Did she . . . die?" the warrior asked.

The boy shook his head. "No, she's fine!" he said. "She doesn't wear these anymore. She told me to donate them to someone who needs them, and that's what I'm doing."

The warrior said, "I need nothing. And I can't accept these, anyway."

"Why not? It's the least I can do."

"The least you can do is leave and never come back."

"Please," he said.

"All right, if it will make you leave me alone." She wrapped up the clothes, nodded at him, and walked away with his gift. "Next time you enter the woods, you're on your own."

When the boy returned the following year, he was now a young man. He moved quietly through the trees—almost as quietly as the warrior woman—so he avoided any encounters with Grimm until he had nearly reached the center of the forest. Leaves rustled over his head as he paused to refresh himself in a shallow stream. Then he looked up to see three oversized, fearsome black owls fixing him in their deadly stare. They spread their wings, revealing razor-sharp feathers and deadly talons.

The boy drew a long, thin sword, which he had forged himself under the dubious eye of the village blacksmith, who wondered why anyone would hunt with such a weapon when they could use a bow and arrow or a spear. But the boy had crafted his sword with a special purpose: to fight the hate-filled monsters from his nightmares.

The savage bird-creatures dived at him, attacking with claws and thundering away with their powerful wings. While he had *hoped* for the warrior woman to appear, he did not expect it, and indeed she did not come to save him. It was a long, clumsy, bloody battle, but eventually the young man prevailed over two of the beasts. The third swooped at him. Exhausted, he couldn't bring up his sword in time—

Then a brilliant white light flooded the woods. He shielded his eyes, and when the brightness faded, the Grimm was gone. A moment later, the warrior woman appeared.

"What was that light? Where did it go?" he asked.

"You're developing a bad habit," she said.

He sheathed his sword and grinned. Was it just wishful thinking, or was she happy to see him? She was wearing a clean white blouse with a black skirt, sturdy boots, and a dark green cloak. Her hair was pulled back into a ponytail. She held her shortened billhook, the end of the broken handle crisscrossed with red ribbon.

"I knew you'd come to my rescue," he said. "Thank you."

"For what? I didn't do anything."

"Didn't you?" He raised an eyebrow. "You were nearby at least."

"I told you I wouldn't save you this time," she said. "Fortunately you did pretty well on your own."

"Then thanks for watching over me yet again. Not just today, but always. Thanks for protecting all of us, for all these years, without anyone knowing you're responsible for our safety."

"Why do you keep coming back here?"

He looked into her eyes.

She snorted. "Don't tell me you're in love with me."

He blushed. "I brought you food." He offered his backpack to her once more.

"I have food." But she opened the bag and pulled out parcel after parcel. There was honey cake, and strawberry tart, and sweet biscuits. When she unwrapped a stack of fresh-baked cookies, her expression lightened, and her happiness made him happy. She popped a cookie into her mouth and chewed.

"I haven't had anything like this in a long time." She stared at the delicacies spread out around her. He got up to leave as she began her feast.

"Don't come back," she mumbled after him, her mouth full.

"I know," he said.

But of course the young man came back, a year to the day later. This time he made it all the way to the center of the woods, where he found a homely hut and the warrior woman waiting for him outside it, at a small table with two seats, two cups, and a steaming pot of tea.

"Now what do you want?" she asked.

"I was just in the neighborhood and thought I would stop by. Didn't see any Grimm this time."

"I cleared them out of the area this morning." She stretched. "They'll be back. They always come back. But we have some time."

"Some time is all we need." He set down the weapons he carried: a new, better-

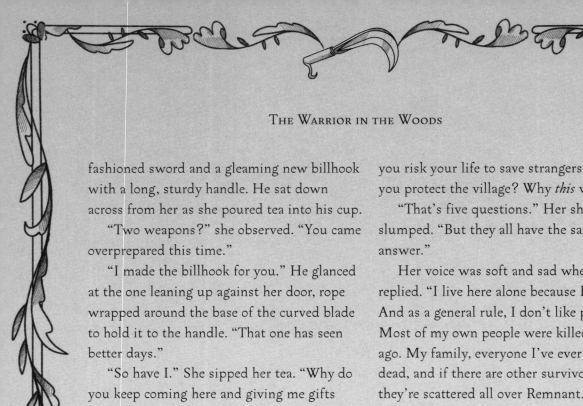

fashioned sword and a gleaming new billhook with a long, sturdy handle. He sat down across from her as she poured tea into his cup.

"Two weapons?" she observed. "You came overprepared this time."

"I made the billhook for you." He glanced at the one leaning up against her door, rope wrapped around the base of the curved blade to hold it to the handle. "That one has seen better days."

"So have I." She sipped her tea. "Why do you keep coming here and giving me gifts every year?"

"You know," he said. "To thank you."

"You've already done that. No need to keep coming back for that."

"You've saved me each time we've met, and maybe more times besides. And I know that you've saved all of us."

She didn't say a word.

He put down his teacup. "May I ask you a question?"

"Ah." She sighed. "Go ahead and ask. I don't promise an answer."

"Nothing is promised in life," he said.

"You've grown up a good deal since I first saw you."

"I had to," he said. "My question is: *Why?* Why do you live in the woods alone? Why do

you risk your life to save strangers? Why do you protect the village? Why *this* village?"

"That's five questions." Her shoulders slumped. "But they all have the same answer."

Her voice was soft and sad when she replied. "I live here alone because I am alone. And as a general rule, I don't like people. Most of my own people were killed long ago. My family, everyone I've ever known is dead, and if there are other survivors like me, they're scattered all over Remnant."

"Killed by Grimm?"

She scowled. "Murdered by other Humans."

"Oh." The young man grasped his cup with both hands, so the tea would warm them. "But then why do you protect others?"

She looked at him steadily. "Because I can. Because no one else will." She smiled. "And because some people are good, like you. And that gives me hope."

She stood, hefted the billhook appreciatively, and walked toward her hut.

"Finish your tea and then go," she said.

But he had more to say. "You've spent all these years looking after us," he explained. "I thought maybe it would be nice if someone looked after you for a change." He stood to

leave. "Because that's what *I* can do. Because no one else will."

She smiled. "Don't come back," she said. But they both knew, by now, that he would.

Over the next year, the village expanded right up to the perimeter of the forest. Then the people went into the forest and chopped down trees to build more houses, so the village grew while the forest shrank. That was the year that the Grimm returned, attacking with more and more frequency and ferocity. People said that the village had broken its promise with the woods. Others suggested that with too many people, there were too many emotions, and that had brought the Grimm back.

But one man knew that the Grimm had always been there, out of sight and out of mind, because the village was protected by a brave warrior. He waited until the appointed day for his annual visit, worried about what he might discover.

It was a nonstop fight to get to her home;

he dispatched wave after wave of Grimm. He paused at each place that he had encountered the woman on his previous visits and waited, but she never appeared. Finally he reached her hut. The bladed staff he had made her was waiting by the entrance, as though she had just stepped away for a moment. But the door was missing, torn off its hinges. The interior was wrecked, whether by man or beast he couldn't tell. It had been abandoned for a while. The warrior woman was gone.

He shouldered the warrior's billhook and fought his way back to the village. Soon, the people would have to leave and settle somewhere else—without their guardian, the woods had become too dangerous. But until that day, he would do his best to protect them in her place. Because he could. Because no one else would.

Back in the village, around a fire that

couldn't quite warm him, he told the people the woman's story, so they would always know who they had to thank for the many good days they'd enjoyed.

"I wish I could have been there for her," he said slowly, "the way she was there for us." If she was dead, she had died alone.

"Why did you keep going back there, year after year?" a village woman asked him. "Because she saved you?"

"For that reason, and for many more," he said slowly. "But I believe she knew the deepest reason of all."

The group waited. He gazed into the fire.

"I fell in love with her the moment I saw her silver eyes."

Ozpin's Notes

More than a few Huntsmen and Huntresses cite this story as one of their childhood favorites, myself included. There are some more fantastical versions of the tale, embellishments which add nothing to its deeper meaning and don't bear repeating—though the least believable element is perhaps the notion that any child could grow up in Remnant without knowing of Grimm, or even encountering them from a very young age. In fact, "The Warrior in the Woods" is often used as a cautionary tale, intended to discourage children from wandering too far from home on their own, or from relying too much on others to save them. But the most enduring, and I think the most inspiring, aspect of this story is one which many have taken to heart: If you can help others, it is your responsibility to do so. Whether that means fighting evil singlehandedly or baking cookies (for kindness can be as rare as silver eyes) is up to the reader to decide for themselves. From each according to their own abilities.

The Man Who Stared at the Sun

By Anonymous

A farmer irrigating his fields at midday exclaimed loudly about the heat. The sun, passing overhead, happened to hear the complaint and replied, "Just as you have your job, I have mine. Rather than criticize, you should thank me! For without my efforts, all of yours would be for naught."

"I work hard to feed my family, and this unbearable heat makes me work even harder." The farmer mopped his sweaty brow with his kerchief. "My crops keep drying up, though I water and tend to them every day. Perhaps you are too good at your job. Instead of me doing more, perhaps you could do a little less."

The sun flared at the suggestion, and the farmer and his crops wilted under the intense heat. The sun began to move on, muttering, "People should accept responsibility for their own failure." But the farmer called after him.

"I'm sorry! You're right. I couldn't do my work without you."

The sun, mollified, cooled off. The farmer sighed with relief. "Thank you," he said.

"That's all I wanted to hear. Everyone is always so quick to blame me, whether it's hot or cloudy, but no one ever bothers to show some appreciation for what I do. They won't even look at me! It really burns me up."

"That's terrible. People should show you more respect and gratitude."

The sun brightened cheerfully.

The farmer squinted. "We are both proud of our jobs and too stubborn to change our ways, but I have an idea to make things better for both of us. How about a race?

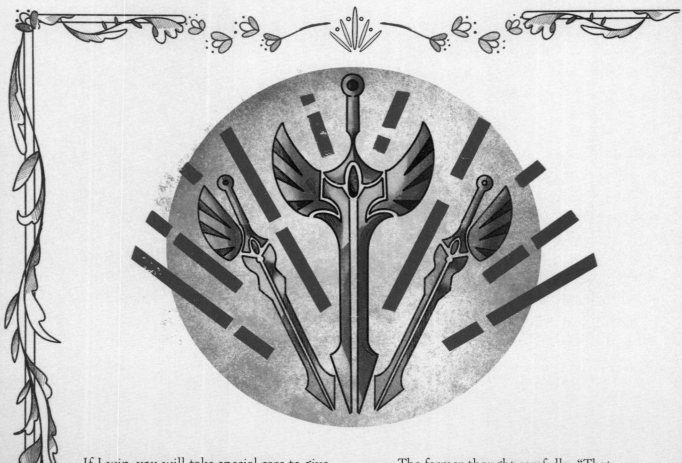

If I win, you will take special care to give my plants just the right amount of light and warmth for optimal growth, for as long as they are tended by my children and my children's children."

"And if I win?"

"I and my children and my children's children will adore you and encourage others to celebrate your magnificence."

"I like this idea," said the sun. "But racing is so exhausting, and we've both been up since dawn. Since you suggested a competition, perhaps I could choose the nature of it?"

The farmer thought carefully. "That seems fair. What will it be?"

The sun smiled. "A staring contest."

"Oh." The farmer hesitated. "Very well."

"Let us begin."

The farmer slowly lifted his face toward the sun, eyes wide open, and the sun fixed its gaze on him. As the hours passed, stinging sweat trickled into the farmer's eyes, but he never flinched and never blinked.

Evening arrived, though it was still bright as day. The farmer's wife came looking for him and was astonished to find him competing with the sun. She begged

her husband to come home to dinner. He refused.

"Look how upset you've made her," the sun said. But the farmer didn't glance away.

"Nice try," said the farmer's wife. She gave her husband some food and then took over his work in the fields.

Days passed, and the sun stayed in place, watching the farmer as the farmer watched him. The farmer's wife and children continued watering the fields around him and their crops flourished from the sun's attention.

"I bet watching your children so hard at work would fill you with pride," the sun said.

"I am proud whether I can admire them or not." Tears trickled down the farmer's cheeks, but he never glanced away and never blinked.

Weeks passed, and while the farmer's fields thrived and the surrounding region grew lush and green, other crops around the world were dying, deprived of light. For the first time, the sun was failing to do his job.

"Your farm has never been more prosperous!" the sun said. "Look around you and marvel at its beauty."

"I cannot," the farmer said sadly. "I'll just take your word for it."

Finally, the tug of duty became too great, so the sun relented. He blinked. "You win. I must carry on with my responsibilities."

The farmer closed his eyes and covered them with a hand. "Remember our agreement," he said wearily.

"As promised, from now on, your crops will grow better than anyone else's, for as long as you and your people work hard and take care of the land."

"Thank you," the farmer said, and this time he meant it.

As the sun began to set, he called back to the man. "I knew you would have beaten me in a race, because I've seen you run faster than the wind."

The farmer shrugged. His Semblance allowed him to cross great distances in the blink of an eye. It was useful in managing his expansive farmlands, and whenever he could get away he loved to travel all over Sanus to take in the continent's wonders.

"That's why I chose a staring contest," the sun said. "Most people cannot bear to look at me for more than a few seconds, so I was sure you would lose right away. I have to know: How did you outlast me?"

The man opened his vacant eyes and said,

23

"I'll tell you. From the start of our competition, I was immediately blinded by your splendor. With the damage already done, I kept my eyes open and faked it."

The sun was angry that he had been tricked after all. But since the farmer had lost so much—he could no longer see his beautiful family, look proudly upon his farm, or race around exploring the world—the sun moved on and honored their bargain.

One can only succeed when one is willing to sacrifice something important.

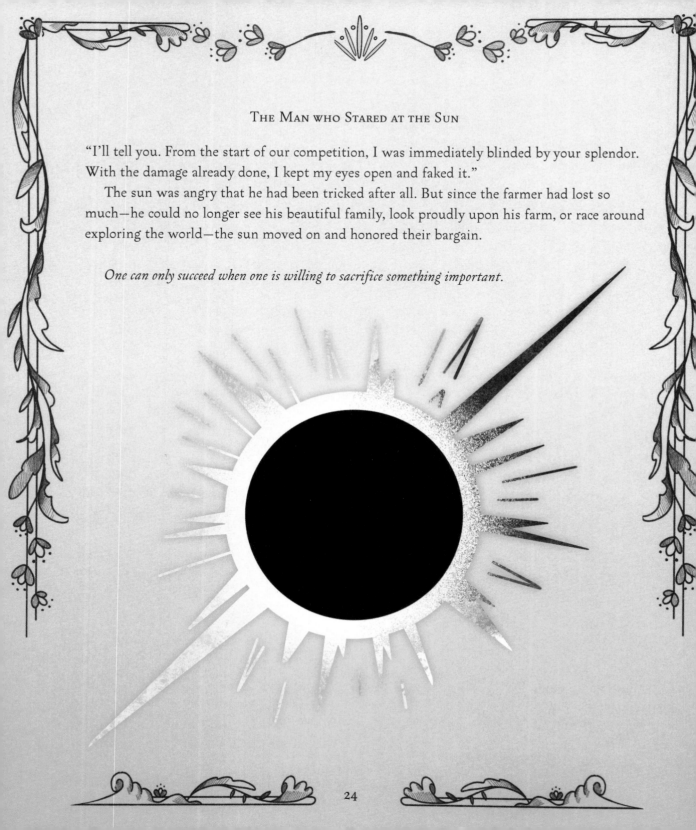

OZPIN'S NOTES

The origins of "The Man Who Stared at the Sun," often called "The Farmer and the Sun," trace back to Vacuo, which of course was once much more verdant than it is now. One variation on the tale makes the farmer a blind man from the beginning, who tricks the unwitting sun into entering a staring contest with him and easily wins; this version has grown in popularity in Vacuo over the years, perhaps reflecting the increased value of ingenuity to survive there. The way the story is told may reveal much about the character of the person telling it. Personally, I think the original version more closely represents the hardy spirit of Vacuo, as the farmer stubbornly makes the most of a bad situation. I am particularly fond of yet another alternate take which offers a simpler, yet classically Vacuan twist on the moral lesson: *Don't stare at the sun.*

The Shallow Sea

SOURCE: TRADITIONAL

Long ago, before the fish had scales, before the birds had feathers, and before the turtles had shells, when our god still walked and crawled and slithered the earth, there were only Humans and animals. (And Grimm. There have always been Grimm. There will always be Grimm. But those creatures don't figure in *this* story, so just put them out of your mind, if you can.) The Humans lived everywhere across Remnant excepting one small island, which our sagacious, perspicacious, and most veracious god protected as a haven for animals of all kinds.

As I hope you will recall, little one, the God of Animals takes whatever form they like, whenever they like. They might be a strong-headed ram in one moment, and a skittering skink the next. Or perhaps a broad-winged roc and then—as quick as a blink—a fierce lion! Or, of course, any combination of any beasts under the sun, so that they might have the head of a lamb, the body of a boar, the feet of an elephant, and the wings of a wyvern. Their form shifts like a changing thought, like flowing water, and if you look away—remember, you should never look away from a god—you might miss a beautiful blending that will never exist again.

Anyway. The God of Animals cantered and burrowed and fluttered over the earth, admiring the creatures they had gathered on this island and seeing that it was good. But the thing about sagacious, perspicacious, and indeed veracious beings is that they tend to get bored. And despite the excellent company

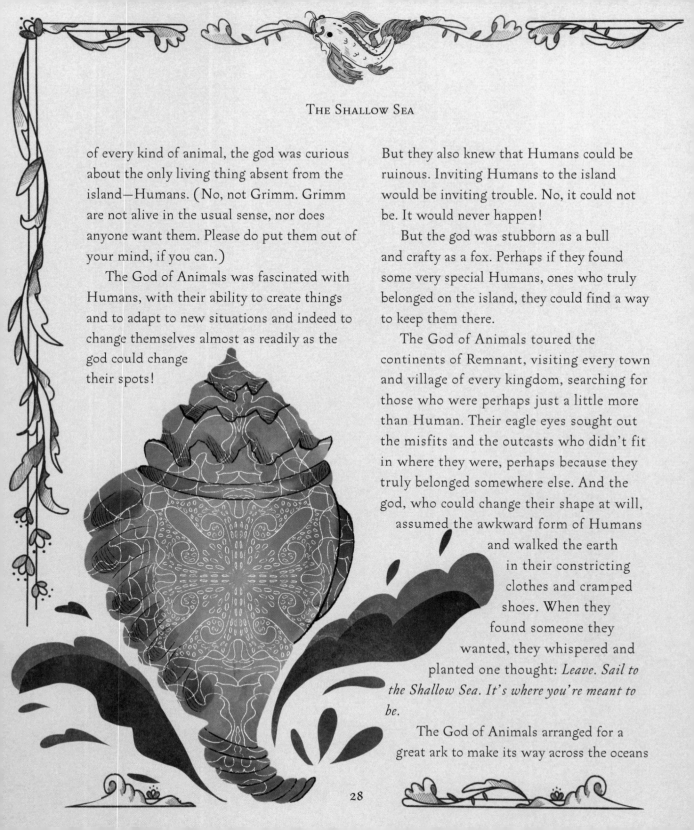

of every kind of animal, the god was curious about the only living thing absent from the island—Humans. (No, not Grimm. Grimm are not alive in the usual sense, nor does anyone want them. Please do put them out of your mind, if you can.)

The God of Animals was fascinated with Humans, with their ability to create things and to adapt to new situations and indeed to change themselves almost as readily as the god could change their spots!

But they also knew that Humans could be ruinous. Inviting Humans to the island would be inviting trouble. No, it could not be. It would never happen!

But the god was stubborn as a bull and crafty as a fox. Perhaps if they found some very special Humans, ones who truly belonged on the island, they could find a way to keep them there.

The God of Animals toured the continents of Remnant, visiting every town and village of every kingdom, searching for those who were perhaps just a little more than Human. Their eagle eyes sought out the misfits and the outcasts who didn't fit in where they were, perhaps because they truly belonged somewhere else. And the god, who could change their shape at will, assumed the awkward form of Humans and walked the earth in their constricting clothes and cramped shoes. When they found someone they wanted, they whispered and planted one thought: *Leave. Sail to the Shallow Sea. It's where you're meant to be.*

The God of Animals arranged for a great ark to make its way across the oceans

of Remnant. It docked at each kingdom and picked up those Humans who longed for a change, or felt they weren't welcome among their own people, or had never felt comfortable in their own skin. The ark loaded with these chosen people sailed down, down, down to the Shallow Sea. And when it reached the sea, it sailed around the island. The people grew uneasy as they observed a harsh desert stretching from the coast as far as the eye could see. They became unsettled as they took note of the diverse wildlife along the shores.

(Were you wondering whether there were any Grimm on the island in those days? As I've told you, Grimm do not figure into *this* story, and I wish you would clear them from your mind.)

"This barren land is no place for us. We should turn back," the people said.

"I want you to see all of this land for what it is," the God of Animals said. "Trust me: You do belong here, if you are willing to work for it."

But then the ark rounded the cape to the southern shore, and the Humans saw that there it was a paradise. The god leapt from the ark and splashed into the water, which reached only to their waist. As they stood there, they shed their Human form and took on the horns of a ram, the tail of a monkey, the scales of a serpent.

"This can be your home, if you want it. You're right, this is no place for mere Humans—but you are no mere Humans. If you jump from the boat and join me, you will see."

The people with the strongest faith leapt from the boat immediately and splashed in the shallow water toward the shore. Those who stayed behind on the boat watched their brethren transform before their eyes, each of them acquiring an animal trait: ram horns, rabbit ears, cat ears, monkey tails, and more. By the time they reached land, they were something new to Remnant—both Human and animal at the same time.

"This land is no less hospitable than where we came from," the people on the beach said. "But here at least we have control of our fates, free from the influence of others."

More people on the boat, emboldened by the miracle they had witnessed, jumped next into the water. They followed the others to the shore of the island, each of them changing in the process, taking on animal features of their own: leopard spots, lion manes, lamb ears, pig snouts, crocodile scales, and more.

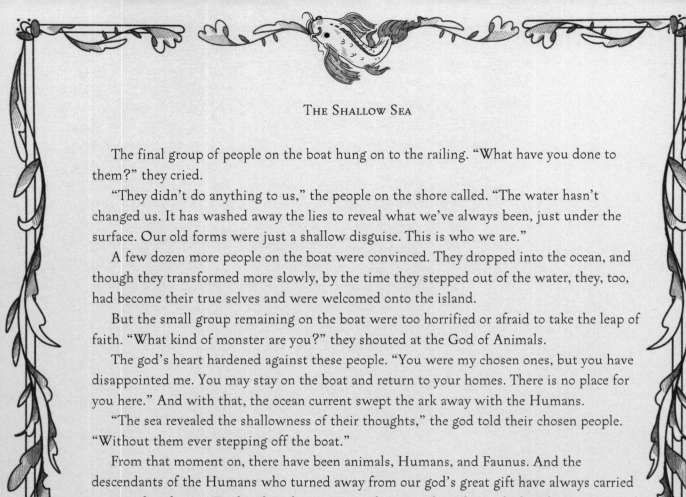

The Shallow Sea

The final group of people on the boat hung on to the railing. "What have you done to them?" they cried.

"They didn't do anything to us," the people on the shore called. "The water hasn't changed us. It has washed away the lies to reveal what we've always been, just under the surface. Our old forms were just a shallow disguise. This is who we are."

A few dozen more people on the boat were convinced. They dropped into the ocean, and though they transformed more slowly, by the time they stepped out of the water, they, too, had become their true selves and were welcomed onto the island.

But the small group remaining on the boat were too horrified or afraid to take the leap of faith. "What kind of monster are you?" they shouted at the God of Animals.

The god's heart hardened against these people. "You were my chosen ones, but you have disappointed me. You may stay on the boat and return to your homes. There is no place for you here." And with that, the ocean current swept the ark away with the Humans.

"The sea revealed the shallowness of their thoughts," the god told their chosen people. "Without them ever stepping off the boat."

From that moment on, there have been animals, Humans, and Faunus. And the descendants of the Humans who turned away from our god's great gift have always carried envy in their hearts. To this day, they resent us for reminding them of what they are not and what they never can be.

Ozpin's Notes

Although this fable once was among the most common stories told to Faunus children, it has never been written down before its appearance here, not by Faunus and certainly not by Humans. I gave serious consideration as to whether to include it, but as it provides a lovely, and I think necessary, counterpoint to "The Judgment of Faunus," also in this collection, I felt it important to record. I humbly request forgiveness if I am perceived to have overstepped myself in any way; know simply that I deeply respect the rich history of Faunus and wish to represent them among stories of Remnant. As Faunus stories are generally passed down from generation to generation, few outsiders have ever heard them, and that does everyone a disservice. We must be exposed to the stories of people from all kingdoms and cultures, Humans and Faunus alike, if we hope to make progress in understanding one another.

That said, we must take care not to characterize "The Shallow Sea" as a mere story, for it is so much more to Faunus. I do not wish to subject it to the literary critiques I might bring to another tale. This story is a key to Faunus's identity, and therein lies its chief value. However, I will note that many Humans and even Faunus view this story as mere fantasy, a fanciful creation myth—and even, perhaps, a dangerous one. In the aftermath of the Great War, when Faunus settled on Menagerie, the story of a magical island made just for them has become tinged with bittersweet irony. Consequently, the story has fallen out of favor and I understand it is rarely spoken these days. This, too, influenced my decision to record it before it is lost to posterity.

Here I will remind you that this story—dare I say every story ever told—may still hold a kernel of truth, even if the plot details are contrived. Whatever the criticisms laid upon "The Shallow Sea," in my opinion it still holds deep truths about Humans and Faunus that everyone should take the time to consider.

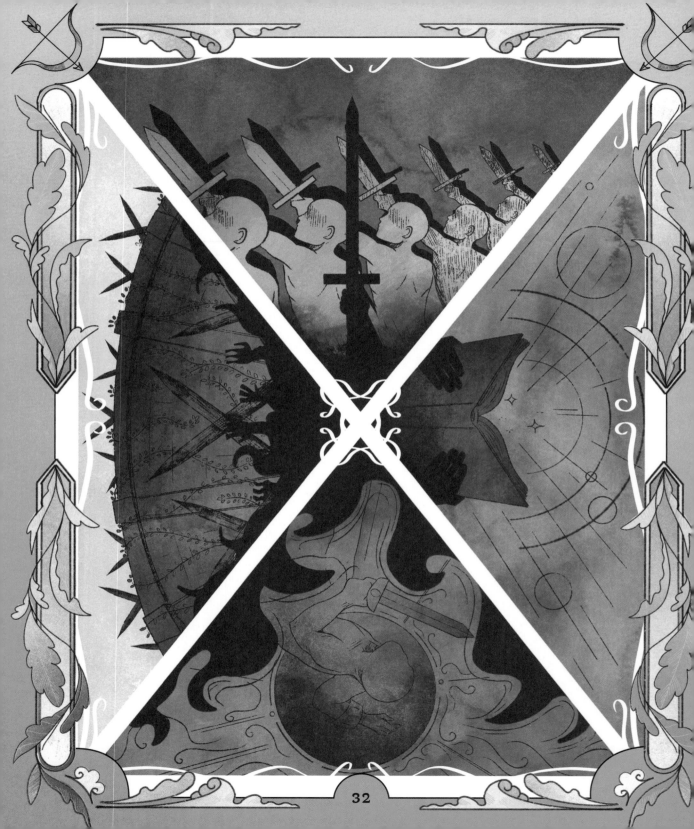

The Hunter's Children

RECORDED BY DOCTOR BARTHOLOMEW OOBLECK

There was once a hunter who had four children: two daughters and two sons. The family lived in a small village deep in the swamps of the kingdom of Mistral, swamps that were also home to fearsome Creatures of Grimm such as the great Lagartodiles, fierce Grendels, poisonous Long Tongues, and tricky Whisps. In those days, if Humans could not defend themselves from Grimm—and they rarely could—they would flee their homes and rebuild what they could of their lives elsewhere. Thus, they left more and more of their land to the monsters . . . and sooner or later the monsters always followed.

However, this hunter was different from all others. Each day, while the other men and women of the village chased swamp animals for food, this hunter chased Grimm. In the evenings, when the men and women came home with meat for their families, this hunter always returned empty-handed. When a Creature of Grimm is killed, its body fades like a bad dream, and you would not want to eat one even if you could.

The hunter and his children did not starve because the other villagers shared their food in gratitude for his protection. While the hunter's family ate dinner, he told his two daughters and two sons about the Grimm he had fought that day and how he had killed them. Often his children asked, "But why are you the only one who hunts them?"

The hunter had several answers for this question, depending on his mood.

"Because my Aura is stronger than anyone else's in the village," the hunter might answer. Which would prompt a lecture about how a strong Aura was not enough on its

own, if one did not know how to use it to shield oneself from harm or activate a Semblance.

"Because my Semblance tells me when Grimm are near," the hunter might answer. This would prompt a lively discussion about who in the family had the most useful Semblance: the older sister, whose Semblance always led her toward what she needed most? The older brother, whose Semblance linked people's Auras as long as they were in physical contact? The younger sister, whose Semblance calmed any Human or animal? Or the younger brother, whose Semblance allowed him to hide in plain sight?

"Because I hate the Grimm for killing your mother," the hunter might answer. "And I hate myself for not being there when she died." Dinner conversation was silent on those nights until one child would ask softly, "Tell us about Mother again." And soon they would be sharing their favorite memories of her, such as her sharp sense of humor, her beautiful singing voice, and her gentle but firm hand in guiding their combat training.

One day, the hunter did not come home from the swamp. The men and women of the village, with fear and pity in their hearts, told the hunter's children that he had died defending them from Grimm. The hunter's two daughters

and two sons grieved that night, but in the morning they sat down to decide what to do.

"We must stay here and defend our home as Father did," the older daughter said.

The older brother said, "What about all the other people out there in need? We must try to help them, too."

"No," said the younger sister. "We need to study the Grimm, so we can figure out better ways to protect against them."

The younger brother shook his head. "We should seek adventure on our own. We know how to fight, but we only put ourselves at risk when we try to protect others."

The hunter's children loved one another too much to argue. Recognizing that they were at an impasse, they decided to split up and pursue their own destinies in their own ways.

The older sister bid her siblings farewell as they departed the following morning. She pledged her services to the village, but the people were upset by the death of the hunter and the Grimm began attacking almost daily. The older sister saved many lives, but the number of Grimm grew while the number of villagers dwindled. Soon many left in search of new homes.

The older brother journeyed to the next village over in search of other hunters like his

father, but that village was gone—destroyed by Grimm. This was also the fate of the next three villages he visited. The fifth village he found under siege. The older brother convinced the villagers to link themselves together with a rope, and supported by their combined Auras, he defeated the Grimm. The villagers welcomed the newcomer as their champion and begged him to stay.

The younger sister ventured into the woods near her village and built a structure high on a tree branch from which she could observe Grimm safely. Whenever one came near, she calmed herself enough to avoid its attention while she made careful notes and sketches. But studying the Grimm in this passive state did not provide useful information about their strength and abilities in combat. One day, a large group of Grimm stormed past in a frenzy. She followed the pack toward whatever was drawing them deeper into the woods.

The younger brother, for all his bravado and independence, had never been in the forest alone before, and he became lost almost as soon as he left home. Though he also could hide from Grimm by closing his eyes, they still sensed his presence—and he was unable to see where he was going. He wandered among the trees for days, feeling frustrated and foolish and

very sorry for himself. Eventually the Grimm trapped him in a clearing, where he huddled on the ground, eyes shut, as they circled.

Suddenly an overwhelming sense of calm came over him and he dared to open his eyes. The nearby Grimm had lost interest in him and began to wander off. Then he heard a familiar voice.

"How's your adventure going, Brother?" the younger sister said.

When he saw her, he jumped up and they embraced warmly. They had never been apart for more than half a day before going their separate ways.

The brother admitted that he had gotten lost in the forest and had been too afraid to fight the Grimm alone. His sister related that she had been studying the Grimm when they suddenly went on the move. They both knew what that meant: Someone else was going to be in trouble soon.

"We have to help them," they agreed. No longer drawn to the brother, the creatures headed off toward a larger target with the reunited siblings following close behind.

A short distance away, the older sister was using her Semblance to lead her village toward what she assumed was a new and safer home. Ever vigilant, she was the first to spot the group

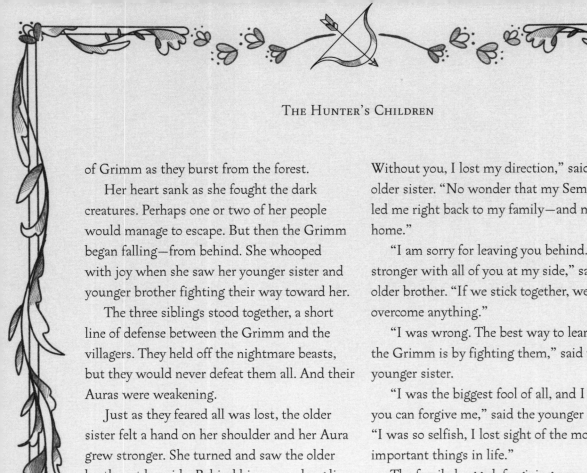

of Grimm as they burst from the forest.

Her heart sank as she fought the dark creatures. Perhaps one or two of her people would manage to escape. But then the Grimm began falling—from behind. She whooped with joy when she saw her younger sister and younger brother fighting their way toward her.

The three siblings stood together, a short line of defense between the Grimm and the villagers. They held off the nightmare beasts, but they would never defeat them all. And their Auras were weakening.

Just as they feared all was lost, the older sister felt a hand on her shoulder and her Aura grew stronger. She turned and saw the older brother at her side. Behind him was a long line of people all tied to a rope at their waists.

"Miss me?" he asked.

The four siblings grinned at one another and clasped hands, renewing their strength. The older brother passed the rope to his siblings, and they looped it about their waists. Linked to the Auras of dozens of people, they were able to destroy the small army of Grimm.

When the fight was won and the night ended, the siblings at last had a chance to catch up.

"I am sorry for being stubborn. There were too many Grimm for me to fight alone.

Without you, I lost my direction," said the older sister. "No wonder that my Semblance led me right back to my family—and my true home."

"I am sorry for leaving you behind. I am stronger with all of you at my side," said the older brother. "If we stick together, we can overcome anything."

"I was wrong. The best way to learn about the Grimm is by fighting them," said the younger sister.

"I was the biggest fool of all, and I hope you can forgive me," said the younger brother. "I was so selfish, I lost sight of the most important things in life."

The family hugged, forgiving one another for their mistakes.

"Father was killed because he was fighting the Grimm alone," the younger sister said. "We work much better as a team."

They all agreed. For the rest of their days, the hunter's children defended the new village they built together, and welcomed anyone seeking refuge from the Grimm. And often over the years, the siblings ventured out into the world to offer help wherever they could, inspiring others with their bravery, heart, wisdom, and humility.

Ozpin's Notes

This is one of my favorite fairy tales, and I include it here not only because its messages still resonate today—perhaps more than ever—but also because the hunter's four children bear a striking resemblance to the four-student teams at each of our Huntsmen academies. One wonders if the king of Vale had this story in mind when he established them after the Great War. While we do not know the exact origin of this tale, it certainly predates the earliest notions of Huntsmen and Huntresses as we now know them—as hunters of Grimm.

The hunter's children also embody many of the traits that make for a good Huntsman, and in my experience, I can vouch for the effectiveness of teamwork in overcoming any obstacle. I have also wondered over the years if the lessons learned by each of the children might also serve as a guide for leaders of Vale, Vacuo, Mistral, and Atlas. Surely four kingdoms, working together, can accomplish more than each of them alone.

The Indecisive King
(a.k.a. The King, the Crown, and the Widow)

SOURCE: ANONYMOUS

Once upon a time, there was a very wise king. Every morning, he opened the gates of his castle to the people of his kingdom and held an open court, where the people could ask for advice, make formal complaints, or petition for his help. The only requirement for seeking an audience with the king was that afterward you had to do whatever he directed.

"My neighbor's tree fell on my fence and broke it," one man reported. "Half of the tree is still lying on my property! Who should pay to remove it and repair my fence?"

"That's an easy one," the king said. "The half of the tree that lies on your property now belongs to you. You will cut up the tree together and both of you will use the wood to rebuild your fence. Sell the remaining wood and split the profits evenly."

"Sounds fair," said the man. "Thank you, Your Grace."

"I'm not finished," said the king. "Use your portion of the sales to purchase a new tree and plant it with your neighbor in place of the one they lost."

The man sighed, but the king was very wise.

On another day, a sad woman in tattered clothes approached the king. "Your Grace," she said. "Creatures of Grimm destroyed my village. My family is dead. Everything I've ever cared about is gone."

"I'm very sorry for your loss." The king stepped down from his throne and clasped the hands of the forlorn widow. "What is your question?" he asked softly.

"What should I do now?"

He studied her face for a long while. He smiled sadly. "You must keep living."

The widow had no choice but to listen to

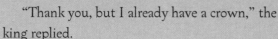

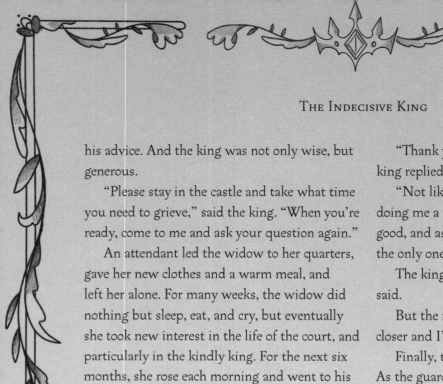

his advice. And the king was not only wise, but generous.

"Please stay in the castle and take what time you need to grieve," said the king. "When you're ready, come to me and ask your question again."

An attendant led the widow to her quarters, gave her new clothes and a warm meal, and left her alone. For many weeks, the widow did nothing but sleep, eat, and cry, but eventually she took new interest in the life of the court, and particularly in the kindly king. For the next six months, she rose each morning and went to his court to watch him dole out advice and justice. The widow admired his steady gentleness and perception. He always saw the truth of a situation, and he listened not only to people's words but also to their hearts.

It happened that the king's grateful subjects sometimes brought him offerings, from food they had prepared to livestock or precious jewels and gold. The king, ever humble, always encouraged others to give to those truly in need, but he was also gracious and polite. It didn't hurt to accept their gifts and then donate them to a good cause himself. One day, a man with wild eyes arrived with a burlap sack that held a gift for the king. When it was his turn to speak, he pulled a silver crown from the sack.

"Please take this, My Grace," the man said.

"Thank you, but I already have a crown," the king replied.

"Not like this one. Believe me, you will be doing me a favor by taking it. It does me no good, and as the wisest king in the land, you are the only one suited to wear it."

The king demurred. "You flatter me," he said.

But the man insisted. "Allow me to come closer and I'll explain."

Finally, the king gestured the man forward. As the guards watched anxiously, the man leaned in and whispered in the king's ear. The king raised an eyebrow.

"How came you to have this?" the king asked.

"That doesn't matter. Will you accept?"

"Very well. It's a hard offer to refuse, and you have made me curious."

The king allowed the man to place the crown on his head. It fit him perfectly, and he closed his eyes.

A moment later, the king snatched the crown from his head and leapt from his seat. His face was pale as the moon.

"What is this?" he cried. "Guards! Seize that man!"

But the man had disappeared.

"Find him," the king spluttered. He collapsed back into his throne and turned the

crown over and over in his hands. "It can't be true," he muttered.

Then he placed the crown back on his head and stared off into the distance.

"Your Grace?" an attendant asked. "There are still a dozen supplicants seeking audience."

The king would not respond, and the attendants dismissed them, along with the entire court. "Sorry," they said. "It's best to come back tomorrow."

As they were led out of the chamber, the widow glanced back at the king on the throne. His brow was furrowed in concentration.

The next morning, the king wandered into court late, for the first time that anyone could remember. Dark smudges under his bleary eyes suggested he had not slept. Though the crown was nowhere to be seen, the king was distracted and behaving oddly as he entertained questions from the court.

"Your Grace," a man said. "My daughter wants to marry her childhood best friend, but he is the son of bakers. I had hoped she would marry higher than her station. What should I do?"

The king shifted in his seat. "Are the boy's parents good bakers?"

The man frowned. "I suppose so. Yes."

"Then what more can you ask for? Let your daughter be happy, and enjoy free bread."

"I hadn't thought of that. Thank you, Your Grace."

A moment later the king waved the man back. "Wait a moment! Perhaps I was wrong. A family requires more than bread. You should follow your instincts and wait for a better match for your daughter."

"What?" the widow said. She clapped her hands over her mouth, but she wasn't the only one who was surprised.

"All right. If you're sure . . ." The man looked around the court in confusion.

"Of course I'm sure. I'm your king." The king clapped. "Next!"

The court murmured.

"What's wrong?" the widow asked a servant. "He's never changed his mind before."

"Or given bad advice," the servant added.

"So you agree that was bad advice?" the widow asked eagerly.

Suddenly nervous, the servant muttered, "Of course not. He's the

king," and hurried away.

The king continued to second-guess himself, his advice increasingly erratic, until he jumped up and rushed out of the chamber without even dismissing the court.

The next day was much the same, as was the next. A red crease marked the king's forehead, and he became ever more sullen and preoccupied.

Then one morning, the court was closed altogether.

"What's going on?" the widow asked.

"The king is no longer accepting audiences with his subjects," an attendant answered.

"Is he all right?" the widow asked with concern.

"He is the king," the attendant said.

The widow threw up her hands in exasperation. "What kind of an answer is that?"

Soon the king's court announced that he was seeking the wisest philosophers in the land to consult with him. The person who helped him would receive their heart's desire. Would-be advisers flocked to the castle for a chance to give the king advice for a change. The only rule was that if they breathed a word about his dilemma,

they would be executed.

"That doesn't sound like the king," the widow said. "He is a good man."

"People change," the king's steward said.

"This all started with that crown," the widow said. "Where is it?"

"Locked away in the bowels of the castle. He has the only key to the room," the steward said. "The king spends most of his time there. It's the first place he goes after speaking to these advisers of his." The steward sniffed. "He never even talks to *me* anymore."

"What could make him so strange and paranoid?" the widow asked. The question had been plaguing her.

"Even if I knew, I wouldn't tell you," the steward said. "On threat of death."

The widow wandered the lower levels of the castle until she found the one door that was locked. She listened at the door but no one was inside. She peered through the keyhole until she spied a wooden chair with the crown upon it.

"That's no throne for a king," she murmured. She hid in the empty room across from it and waited. She did not have to wait long. The king had an audience with an adviser

42

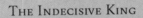

that morning, and he soon came hurrying down to the room. He looked around suspiciously before drawing a key from a chain around his neck and opening the door. He closed it tightly behind him.

The widow crept up to the door and peered through the keyhole. The king sat on the wooden chair, the crown on his head. His head was bowed, as though the crown had grown too heavy for him to lift. He murmured to himself, then suddenly pulled the crown from his head and threw it across the room. He hurried over to pick it up and then placed it back on the chair with care.

The widow took a deep breath. She stood and knocked on the door.

The door flew open. The king's face was contorted with rage. He seized her arm. "Who are you? What are you doing here?" He called out to the hallway, "Guards!"

The widow raised a hand protectively. "Your Grace. Half a year ago I came to you with a question."

"I don't remember," he said.

She swallowed her disappointment.

"You told me to come back when I was ready and ask my question again," she said.

"I don't give out advice anymore," the king said, sighing. "I can barely help myself."

The widow's voice was firm. "I am not here to ask for your wisdom, but to offer some of my own. You called for people to come and advise you on your problem. I am here to make my attempt."

"You?" He shook his head, but she persisted.

"Tell me what's troubling you. Whatever it is, it is too much for one person to bear, and we need our king back."

The king considered. Then he nodded. "This crown has shown me a vision of a crossroads in my future. I will have an important decision to make one day, and from what I can tell, an impossible one. I can't see my way to a favorable outcome. This has never happened to me before."

"Not all outcomes are favorable, My Grace," the widow said.

"I can't accept that. This crown has given me time to figure it out. To work out a solution."

"This crown has burdened you with a problem that you are not yet able to handle. That perhaps you will never be able to handle. In the meantime, it has paralyzed you with indecision. Even if you come up with an answer, you will have more time to wonder if it's the correct one. If such a thing exists."

The king frowned.

"If you can't make simple decisions now— whether a girl should marry a baker or if two

people claiming ownership of the same pig should divide it in two—then how will you respond when the moment of decision finally comes? If it ever comes?" The widow picked up the crown. "This is no gift. It is a curse."

"What should I do?" the king asked.

The widow smiled. "You must keep living."

The king collapsed into the rickety old seat. "That's good advice." He sighed.

"You gave me that advice. But you also gave me more than that. You gave me my life. Hope for a future. And soon afterward . . ." Her face flushed. "A reason for living."

She held up the crown. "May I?"

He held up a hand. "You don't want to do that."

"You'll forgive me if just this once I ignore your excellent wisdom." She placed the crown on her head.

The widow saw a future moment, a decision posed by the man before her. Only he seemed different than he did now—happier. And he looked at her differently than he did now. He asked her a question. She didn't need any time to consider her answer.

"Yes," she breathed.

"'Yes' what?" the kng asked when she removed the crown.

"Let's wait and discover that question together," she said. "I imagine my vision was rather different from yours."

"Excuse me?" the king asked.

"Forget it." She placed the crown on the ground and resisted the urge to stomp on it. "If you want my honest advice, I would lock this crown in here and throw away the key. Put it out of your mind. Live your life, and trust in yourself to make the right decision when the moment comes, with all the information you have at hand." She shrugged. "Or allow yourself to make the wrong decision, comforted in the knowledge that you tried your very best. In either case, the future is one of your own making."

The king smiled. "Allow myself to make a mistake?"

She took his hand and pulled him to his feet. "Just as you gave me permission to go on living, even when my life had changed forever."

"I think I do remember you," he said again.

"Good," she said. It was a start.

Once upon a time, there was a very wise king. And an even wiser queen.

This is just one example of many fairy tales that feature magical items that can help or harm their owners—or maybe both at the same time. These are usually cautionary tales, demonstrating that the curtain separating good and evil is thin indeed. They also underscore an unfortunate but all too common truth: Bad things sometimes happen to good people.

We all acknowledge that knowledge is power, but the wise king in this story learns, with a little help, that *too much* knowledge can make you powerless. Whether you are dealing with knowledge, power, or a mystical artifact, what matters most is what you choose to do with it. Or what you don't choose.

Even the darkest stories may offer comfort, and I find the message of this tale somewhat uplifting: No matter what life deals you, no matter how hard the decisions you must face, keep living.

The Grimm Child

SOURCE: TRADITIONAL

o on, I double-dare you," Poppy said. She nudged her younger brother, Oak, toward the forest edge. But he planted his feet and refused to budge.

"Mother and Father forbid us from entering the woods," Oak said firmly.

Poppy threw up her hands. "Oh, it isn't dangerous. You're just a coward." She saw no need to worry about her parents' rules.

"I want to go home," Oak whimpered, his lips trembling.

She retorted, "It's perfectly safe! Look, I'll go in first." So she did.

Poppy darted into the forest, ignoring Oak's wailing. She didn't go far, though. She slipped behind a thick tree trunk and watched her brother cry. He huddled on the ground not ten feet away, arms around his knees as he rocked back and forth, screaming her name.

"Poppy! Poppy! Poppy!"

The coward wasn't even going to come after her to see if she was all right. He was utterly useless, she thought.

Then suddenly Oak stopped yelling. Poppy could still see him, but he had gone quiet. When she looked behind her, the hairs on the back of her neck rose and the shadows seemed somehow closer. She ran out of the forest, but she shoved her shaking hands into her pockets and put on a broad smile when she reached her brother.

"Told you so. Not a single Grimm! Now it's your turn," Poppy said, taunting him.

Oak looked up, wet lines streaking the dirt on his face. Why was he always so dirty?

"I don't want to," he said, pouting.

But Poppy insisted. "It's only fair. I went first, now you have to go. If you don't, I won't be your friend. I won't play with you anymore."

"You have to be my friend," Oak said.

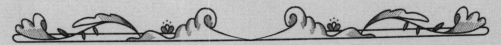

"I have to be your sister. It isn't the same thing," Poppy said. "I have other friends. *Lots* of other friends."

He hated when she played with them and left him behind. So Oak pulled himself to his feet and gave her a miserable look. "Please don't make me," he moaned.

Poppy crossed her arms. Oak sighed and trudged toward the forest, dragging his feet and slowing down as he reached the first line of trees. He turned back once, and Poppy made a shooing motion. Then he walked into the forest until the darkness swallowed him.

Poppy waited for Oak to shriek and run out again. He had always had an active imagination, fueled by occasional accounts of Grimm attacks in Vale. He often woke her up at night, crying over bad dreams. He wouldn't last long inside the forest.

Poppy listened hard for him, but the forest was so silent it was almost unsettling. It was getting dark and cold and their parents would be expecting them home soon. Oak had seemingly vanished.

He's probably just hiding like I did, Poppy thought as she approached the forest once again. *He copies everything I do.*

This time, crossing into the dark web of trees felt like crossing into another world. It was already night here, and the air itself seemed to be breathing all around her. Poppy's skin crawled as she went deeper and deeper into the forest. In the gloom she could barely make out a trail worn into the grass and dirt, or perhaps faded and overgrown with time. Would Oak have walked here? Suddenly she was unsure.

She nearly tripped over him, a lump in the path. He was huddled over like before, head down, arms wrapped around his knees.

Poppy nearly yelled at him, but instead she crouched and put a hand over his. It was ice-cold. He was only a little boy.

"I'm sorry," she said softly. "I shouldn't have made you. Let's go home."

At the word "home," Oak lifted his head. His face was as pale as Grimm bone. He had to be frightened out of his mind, Poppy realized, and she felt a flash of sympathy. She took his hand, helped him up, and led him back the way they'd come.

Her brother was unusually quiet, probably either in shock or sulking, she thought. He gripped her hand tightly in his, fingers digging into her flesh like he would die if he let go, but his skin never warmed.

By the time she got him inside their house, she was really worried. His eyes were glassy and sunken in his pale face, the skin around them

bruised like he hadn't been sleeping. Before their parents spotted him, Poppy hurried Oak to their room and explained that he wasn't feeling well. Mother and Father were angry that they were back so late, but also relieved to see them. Poppy was thankful they would never know that she and Oak had defied their wishes.

She had a cold supper and followed Oak to bed as soon as she could. He was only a round shape under the covers now. When the mound twitched, Poppy said, "Shhhh . . . Go back to sleep." Then, more quietly she added, "I'm sorry about before. I love you."

In the middle of the night, Poppy woke in a cold sweat. Screams echoed in her head, remnants of a forgotten nightmare. She looked at Oak's bed, but his sheets were twisted in a heap on the floor. He was gone.

Poppy slipped out of bed, stepped out of her room, and tiptoed softly through the house, listening for Oak. Her parents' bedroom door was open, and Poppy was relieved. Oak must have gone in there to sleep, which he often did when he woke in the night. Poppy crept to the door and peered in. Her parents were sitting up in bed.

Poppy walked in. "Mother? Father?" Her voice was dry and raspy, almost a whisper. Had she caught a chill in the forest? Her parents didn't respond, so she drew closer. Then she fell back in horror when she saw their faces.

Their mouths gaped and their lifeless eyes were wide open. Their skin had turned as pale as bone. She couldn't bring herself to touch them, but she knew they would be cold as the

Solitas tundra. Poppy huddled on the floor of their room, knees to her chest, paralyzed with fear.

After she had calmed herself, Poppy stood up. She still had to find her brother. "Oak!" she called, passing from room to room. He wasn't there. The front door was open, though, and she went through it into the freezing night. "Oak!"

It was well after midnight, but lights were on next door at the home of her best friend, Lorimar. She walked up to the house and let herself in. Lorimar's parents lay on the ground in the kitchen in the same state as her own parents: white skin, blank eyes. With growing dread, Poppy entered Lorimar's room, where they had been playing cards just the morning before.

Oak was there, slumped over Lorimar's bed, but Poppy's friend was missing.

Oak's hair was now as white as his skin, and red lines radiated up his neck and down his arms. He was cold to the touch. How had he gotten here, and where was her friend?

Poppy felt too numb to weep. She left the house and mechanically went to the next one on the street, where she found a similar scene. Everyone dead. She went to the next, and the next. Five houses down she found Lorimar's body, and another missing child, an older girl named Lily. Lily's body turned up at Dijon's

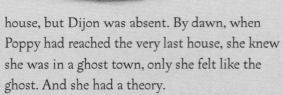

house, but Dijon was absent. By dawn, when Poppy had reached the very last house, she knew she was in a ghost town, only she felt like the ghost. And she had a theory.

She no longer felt anything when she found more bodies, identical to the others. She only felt curiosity and fear when she didn't find Dijon's body. He was out there somewhere, perhaps still in town looking for more victims. What if Poppy was the last person alive? She had to leave.

She hurried back to her house to pack her things. To say good-bye to her dead family and her home. To say she was sorry for bringing this nightmare on all of them, for bringing it back

from the forest, because she was certain it was all her fault. She had goaded her brother into trespassing in the woods, and now she knew he had died there. The thing she had led home with her had been wearing Oak's shape, hiding in his body or controlling it, and waiting to kill the next people who came into its path. Poppy had heard of Grimm that could possess objects like Geists, but possessing Humans? Children? Anything was possible where the darkest of evil was concerned.

Poppy avoided looking at her parents' room as she returned to her own. She flung open her closet, but her suitcase wasn't there and she was overcome with a sense of dread. Suddenly she remembered her own time in the forest, when she was peering out at her brother from the trees. Had she herself come close to being possessed? She had felt a malevolent presence in the forest, after all. She had seen shadows moving in. She had escaped, but Oak had taken her place.

Why not me? she wondered. Why had the Grimm possessed Oak, left her alone, killed her parents, and moved on to Lorimar?

Poppy remembered where she had left her suitcase. It was under the bed! She knelt down and reached for it, groping around until her hands closed around—

Something cold.

She lurched back. *No.*

Forget the suitcase, forget her things. She had to go. Now.

Instead, Poppy slowly lifted the covers that dangled to the floor. Leaned down and peered under.

There was a body.

She swallowed and reached and dragged it out. She already knew who it was, who it had to be. And she knew what that had to mean.

She left Dijon's body there on the floor, and went to the bathroom. She looked in the mirror and saw her own face. Only it wasn't her face anymore.

Her long hair was as white as the snow on a mountaintop, her face as stark as a blank page. Dark veins crept toward her large, black eyes, matching the veins twining her pale arms. She was no longer Poppy. She was dead. She was now a demon.

Perhaps in gratitude, or maybe to torment her with the full knowledge of what she had started the moment she defied her parents and sent her brother into the woods, the Grimm had saved Poppy for last.

The tragic tale of Poppy and Oak is one of the most well-known in this collection, as it has inspired dozens of horror novels, films, comic books, and even video games. Though the names of the characters often change with each telling—thus the use of the more traditional title, "The Grimm Child"—this story has become a staple around campfires and at bedtime. (It is also known to be a special favorite of parents with disobedient children.) Although some of its edginess may have worn off, it continues to serve as a cautionary tale, even for those quick to dismiss it as a children's story. For as with most of the fables in this collection, it contains a grain of truth, and perhaps more than just a grain.

The type of Grimm that Poppy encounters does exist and is popularly called the Chill, at least by the seasoned Huntsmen I have consulted. No matter where this story appears, in whatever form, it always includes some variation on the line "She must have caught a chill in the forest." Whether this line informed the name of the real-life Grimm or vice versa is unknown, but in some written accounts the word is in fact capitalized. Chills are not restricted to hopping from child to child, however—they can possess anyone with the slightest touch. The good news is, they are only found in shadows, and almost always travel alone.

Perhaps you have played the old party game The Chill, in which players must attempt to discover the Grimm in their midst before it is too late, the idea being that a Human possessed by the Chill is indistinguishable from an unpossessed Human. However, you may be relieved

Ozpin's Notes

to know that a Chill in a Human host cannot speak or act normally, the way that Poppy does. If someone has been taken over by a Chill, you would know it immediately; they cannot speak, or perhaps they will only repeat the same word, over and over again—the last word the Human spoke. Moreover, Chills cannot control a Human body for more than a few minutes, making it impossible for them to kill an entire town in one night. They rely on the element of surprise and the unwillingness of most people to kill a friend or loved one until they are certain they are already lost. Small comfort perhaps, for if you are ever unfortunate enough to encounter one, you likely will not survive to tell the tale.

Another important note: The descriptions of the possessed children and dead townspeople in the original tale do not include the white skin and hair or the black eyes. So where did the white hair and skin come from, and why did I choose that particular description for this collection? I believe that over the years some versions of this story have been conflated with another fairy tale about a white witch in the woods, which bears other striking resemblances to "The Grimm Child." Purists may resist my decision not to separate the traditional tales, but this is a case in which the popular version is so familiar and beloved that it has become almost canon. It also fits with our natural inclination to expect and hope that evil will be easy to recognize, rather accepting that evil can lurk behind any face. Alas, we are often slowest to see that darkness within ourselves.

The Judgment of Faunus

RECORDED BY PROFESSOR LEONARDO LIONHEART

Many, many years ago, in a faraway land, there was a war between Humans and animals. Humans envied animals because of all the amazing things they could do: They could run faster than a rumor spreads, see in darkness as if it were daylight, and wield the strength of three people at once. All that, and they were never troubled by the Creatures of Grimm, which sought only to destroy Humans and their creations. The Humans' envy soon turned into hatred.

Yet animals also envied Humans because of all the amazing things *they* could do. Humans could use Dust to perform miracles; they could adapt to any situation; and they could build structures, machines, tools—and weapons. All that, and they persisted in the face of constant adversity and tragedy brought by the Creatures of Grimm. The animals' envy soon turned into fear.

As the war raged on, there were many casualties on both sides. At night, animals raided the Human village and took whatever they needed to survive. During the day, Humans hunted animals in the forest.

One day, a god was passing through the land when they happened upon a bloody fight between the Humans and the animals. They froze everyone in place and walked onto the battlefield.

"Why are you fighting?" the god asked. Their words were understandable to both species, who did not understand each other's language and had never tried to learn. The god released one Human and one animal to answer.

The Human and the animal eyed the god

suspiciously. They had two arms and two legs like a Human, but also branching horns like an animal.

"Are you Human or animal?" the animal asked.

"I am neither and both," the god said. "Why are you fighting?"

"They are not like us," the Human and the animal said, pointing at each other. Little did they know that they had spoken the same words. Fear of those different from you is a universal language.

"Why must everyone be the same?" the god asked them.

"We worry about what they might do to us," the Human and animal said.

"So you have something in common, after all." The god crossed their arms. "Judge not what others might do, but by what you see them do."

"Humans are as capable of destruction as they are of creation," the animal said. "Evil is in their hearts."

"Animals are so much stronger than us, but they will not join us in fighting the Grimm," the Human retorted.

"Have you tried working together?" the god asked.

"Yes," the animal said. "But the Humans wanted to control us and make us their property so they can sacrifice our lives against the Grimm instead of their own. But that is not our fight! We just want to be free."

"Yes," the Human said. "But the animals are wild and unruly. They steal from us at night. We only want to keep them in their place so we may live in safety and peace."

"You have grown to see only the worst in one another," the god said. "But you are more alike than you realize. Your potential is unlimited if you can only learn to celebrate one another's best qualities and embrace your differences."

The god looked around and soon the larger group of Humans and animals could move again. Each side regarded the other apprehensively.

"I can end this conflict if you all agree to subject yourselves to my judgment," the god said. "If you do not agree to live in peace, you will kill one another off, and perhaps destroy the world in the process."

The Humans and animals considered carefully. The Humans saw themselves in the god's speech and manner and were certain the god would side with them. The animals noted the god's magnificent horns, so they assumed the god would side with them.

"We choose life," the Humans and animals said at the same time.

"We accept your judgment, O Wise One."

"So be it," the god said. Suddenly a thick fog rolled onto the battlefield. The Humans and animals called out in panic when they were unable to see one another, still worried that the other side would attack. When the fog finally dissipated, the god was gone—and the Humans and animals were also gone, for when they could see one another again, they could see that both sides had changed. The animals had gained Human features and stood upright on two legs, while the Humans had gained animal features and enhanced senses. Though they all now looked alike, they also were different from one another: Some had the ears of a cat, some the horns of a bull. Some had sharp tusks while others had long tails. Some had strong scales or spikes, some had fins or wings.

"What have you done to us?" they all cried.

"I thought the god was going to judge which of us was superior," one person complained.

"Maybe they have," said one of the animals. "Were you Human or animal before?"

"I don't think it matters anymore," the person admitted.

If you looked closely, you could tell who had been Human, because of the way they stroked their new fur and lifted their eyes to try to glimpse their new horns or held their hands up to admire their new claws.

You could tell who had been animal, because of the way they stumbled and fell on two legs like a newborn, poked at their bare flesh, and pressed their fingers clumsily against their rows of flat teeth. Also, they had no clothes, and they were astonished to feel a strange new emotion—embarrassment— although the idea of dressing up like Humans had never occurred to them before.

"I can see so far!"

"Look at how much I can lift!"

"I have hands!"

"I'm walking on two feet like a monkey!"

Those who had been Human shared their own cloaks and jackets with those who needed coverings.

Finally one of them said what they all could see and feel. "It seems we are neither Human nor animal."

The whole crowd had the same question. "Then what are we?"

"Better than both," one suggested.

The god had created the first Faunus, combining the best parts of both Humans and animals so they could live in peace together. But that is not the end of the story—

rather, it is only the beginning. Solving one problem often creates new ones to deal with, and the Faunus would not live happily ever after. Instead of warring with one another based on jealousy and fear, they would still fight with one another—over matters of philosophy instead of appearance.

As the Faunus acclimated to their new forms and to their new kin, Creatures of Grimm approached the former battlefield stealthily—drawn by the heightened emotions and confusion of the fledgling beings. Those who had been animals were unconcerned at first, as the Grimm had never bothered with them before, but they soon discovered that Grimm were as interested in Faunus as they were in Humans.

Delighting in and emboldened by their newfound strength and agility, creativity and adaptiveness, the Faunus engaged the Grimm in combat. But they were still uncertain in their bodies, unfamiliar in the ways of Aura and Semblances. They took heavy losses against the Grimm, and it was a terrible blow to be cut down before finding their destiny as a new race. Horrified and afraid, the Faunus beat a hasty retreat to the local village. But there they received a poor welcome and faced yet another hurdle.

The villagers closed their doors and their hearts to the strangers, alarmed by their appearance. "We live here," cried some of the Faunus who had previously been Human. "Don't you remember us?"

"We don't know you," cried the villagers, their faces stony and their voices cold. "We don't trust you. Begone!"

"Were we so narrow-minded when we

were Human?" asked a Faunus who had been so.

"Yes," replied the rest.

The Faunus had changed so much, inside and outwardly, so that they were no longer recognizable to their mothers and fathers, sisters and brothers, sons and daughters. In addition, they had been pursued by Creatures of Grimm, which the villagers viewed as an intentional attack. In the chaos that followed, the Faunus and Humans all fled for their lives. The Humans left to find a new settlement, safe from Grimm and closed to Faunus. The Faunus left to find somewhere they could live peacefully with one another and become the best versions of themselves, free of prejudice.

Since they were born, Faunus have never stopped running from Grimm and Humans, and searching for a place to call home.

While this Faunus creation story is just as based in myth as "The Shallow Sea," it contains no less truth; in fact, here the truth lies much closer to the surface.

If the former is a popular bedtime story for Faunus children, this more somber and didactic tale often takes its place as they come into adulthood and learn the harsh realities of the world and Faunus-Human relations. Unsurprisingly, Faunus always cast their god as a wise and noble figure, while Human stories portray the same god as a trickster, not to be trusted. Rather telling, isn't it? Notably, many Faunus fairy tales are open-ended like this one, and it's uncommon to find any that offer what anyone might characterize as a "happily ever after." Quite the contrary: Faunus stories tend to be bittersweet or downright depressing.

If you are familiar with the classic novel *The Thief and the Butcher* (or have seen the excellent film adaptation), you might recognize a common theme in Faunus literature—much of it reflects the Faunus' belief that their story is still unfolding and they have yet to discover their true purpose. This is a fascinating and dare I say *comforting* notion, the idea that we are all the heroes of our stories and that we have yet to make our greatest achievements. I trust that we all will have an important role to play in our shared destiny, Faunus not least among us.

The Infinite Man

RECORDED BY PROFESSOR OZPIN

There once was a man. This man was said to be very powerful. Some claimed that he could perform magic like a god. Some even claimed that he himself was a god, but he was always the first to deny it: "I am only a man. Not even a very good one," he said.

One day, this man happened upon a village under attack by Creatures of Grimm. Most people would hasten past and be glad of their own good fortune, but though he was only a man, he was certainly unlike most people. Instead of quickening his pace and continuing his journey, he entered the village, drawn toward panicked cries for help that may as well have been calling his name.

It was a mistake. But it was not his first, and it would not be his last.

This man stood alone against an army of evil monsters. When the battle was over, every last Grimm in the village had been eradicated, and the man was utterly spent. Four survivors cautiously emerged from their hiding places, wondering how they had been saved. They found the man, unconscious but alive, and nursed him back to health.

He awoke four days later. "Thank you for saving us, stranger," they greeted him. "But how did you defeat all those Grimm by yourself?"

The man said simply, "I have been at this a very long time."

"You could have died!"

"I likely would have, if not for you."

They were surprised. "But we're the reason you got hurt in the first place."

"Were you? Well then, I guess we're even."

"But you didn't have to stop to save us."

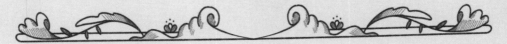

"Of course I did. I was here when no one else could help. Why did you stay behind to take care of me?"

"Because we were here, and you needed us."

The man smiled. "And thus the circle is complete."

"I saw what you did!" A little girl stepped forward, staring at the man with wide eyes. "I was hiding and I saw. You waved your stick, and the monsters turned to ash."

Her adult companions laughed. "She's been going on about this for days. We were hoping you could set her straight."

"It's true," she cried. Tears filled her eyes and her voice shook. "They blew away."

"Now don't tell lies," the adults berated the girl.

"Do not be so quick to dismiss the words of the young," the man said, smiling kindly at the girl. He hesitated a moment, then added, "Especially when they speak the truth."

The villagers were confused. "No Dust can do something like that to Grimm," they said.

"No Dust can," the man agreed.

"Then it must have been magic, and you must be a god."

He held up his hands. "I am only a man. Not even a very good one."

"How can you say that after risking your life for strangers?"

"I'm trying to be a better man." He closed his eyes and appeared to sleep, so the others left him alone to rest. They had more questions than before, but those could wait until morning.

That night, the man crept out of the village. Soon, he realized he was being followed. It was the four villagers he had rescued, along with the girl.

"What do you want?" the man asked.

"We want to be more like you," one of the villagers said. "Maybe we can't learn to do the amazing things you can, but we can learn to try."

The man was moved, and yet he protested. "I travel alone," he said.

"Aren't you lonely?" asked the girl.

The man was lonely indeed, and the girl reminded him of his own family, long gone.

She smiled. "You don't have to be alone anymore." Then she repeated his own words back to him: "'Do not be so quick to dismiss the words of the young.'"

"Especially when they speak the truth," he added, shaking his head. "You are a quick learner." He agreed to let them accompany him, for a little while at least. Until they found a new village where they could settle or he could leave them behind without being noticed.

It was a mistake. And it would not be his last.

The group journeyed together for four years, and in that time, they were joined by more people they'd rescued from Grimm. Word traveled faster than they did, and soon others began seeking them out. Some wanted to learn from the man. Some wanted to be safe. And some just wanted to become part of something bigger than themselves. When people whispered rumors about the man and his followers, they called them the Circle: a fellowship of people committed to learning from, and helping, others for the benefit of all.

"A new group just arrived, from southern Esker," said the girl—now a young woman. "Seven men, nine women, and four children."

"What do they want?" asked the man.

"They want to join your Circle, of course."

He rolled his eyes. "*My* Circle. But it was your idea to call us that."

"People need a name to rally around, and since you won't give us yours . . ."

"I have had many names—"

"So you've said."

He sighed. "This is a dangerous path. I have never wanted acolytes."

She was startled. "Is that all we are to you?" she asked. "I thought we were your friends. I thought you were our family."

His voice softened. "You are that. But I have made terrible mistakes that hurt both those close to me and strangers alike. Those who follow me are likely to find regret or worse. Particularly my . . . family."

"You know, it's talk like that, your humility and unwillingness to lead, that makes people want to follow you. Ironic, isn't it?" she pointed out.

He smiled wryly. "I was thinking more along the lines of 'annoying.'"

"We follow you because we love you and want to learn from you. You are always saying our future depends on people coming together. That is exactly what you are accomplishing here."

"What *we* are accomplishing here," the man said. "You call me your savior, when in truth it is you who saved me."

The young woman blushed. "That's what your teachings are all about. If we can't save ourselves, we have to save one another. Life is a circle, is it not?"

The man laughed. "The student becomes the master. It's also annoying when you throw my words back at me."

"That's why I do it," she said.

"But you're right, as usual. We need to teach as many people as we can to defend themselves,

and protect one another, against the Grimm. And from worse things they might face."

"What could be worse than the Grimm?" she asked.

"I hope you never find out," he said.

Not long after this, the man was poisoned by someone in his own group. When the traitor was discovered, he hissed, "We have heard that the man cannot die. I wanted to see if that was true."

The young woman wanted to execute the traitor, but from his deathbed the man intervened. "Let him go, that he may tell others the truth: I am just a man. And not even—" A cough kept him from finishing.

"A very good one," the young woman said. She let the traitor go.

"Isn't there anything you can do, with all your powers?" the young woman asked the man. "Can't you save yourself?"

She leaned forward. "You told us that your life is a circle and you have lived other lives before this one. That you have had many names. Does that mean that the traitor was right?"

"I talk too much," he whispered.

"So it's true?"

His voice was so low she strained to hear it. "I have never lied to you. But sometimes we make our own truths. We believe what we want to believe, or what we need to believe."

"If you weren't already dying, I would kill you myself. If everything you've said is true, you must promise to come back to me. Come back to us," she begged.

"I can't promise that."

She stroked his forehead, comforting but also cajoling. "All right, all right," she said. "But come back anyway."

When the man died, the Circle mourned him for four days and four nights. But they carried on together and continued spreading the lessons he had taught them. When he did return in a new life and body, he was moved by all they had accomplished. He revealed himself to their leader, now a middle-aged woman.

It was a mistake. And it would not be his last.

"It's really you! You came back!" the woman said.

"You didn't believe me until now?" he asked, disappointed.

"You have to admit, even with everything I saw you do, immortality sounded farfetched."

She caught the man up on all he had missed: The Circle had settled and founded its own town, but they still sent people out to help others and sometimes they brought back new members. Circle was renowned as the

only place with formal training in
defense against the Grimm, mastering
Aura, and unlocking Semblances. It
was said that they created gods
among men.

The man described his
journey back, as he had traveled
much in the way he always had.
But he had heard about the Circle
everywhere he went, and finally he had
to see it for himself. As he spoke to
the woman, an audience gathered,
and soon word spread throughout
the Circle that the founder had
returned. The man rose to leave,
but the woman protested and asked
him to stay. He had built Circle,

and they needed him.

"You clearly do not," he said,
gesturing to the village around them.
"You did all this without me. This
movement has taken on a life of its
own."

"We didn't do this without you,"
the woman argued. "You were the
foundation for everything, and
your presence will make us even
stronger."

The others cheered in
agreement. The man considered.
He had wanted to bring people

together, and his efforts were finally bearing fruit. The accidental experiment was working, far better than any attempts he had planned in his previous lifetimes.

"The people here believe in magic, though many have never seen it," she said. "If you show everyone that it's real, that the man with infinite lifetimes has returned as he promised—"

"I never promised," the man said. "And any charlatan can show them magic, if that's all they're interested in."

She shook her head. "We trust in you and the fate you've laid out for us. We believe in the good of people and our shared responsibility to protect one another and Remnant. So many have heard our stories about you, but now you're here, in the flesh. Your presence is living proof that everything you've said is true. It reinforces our beliefs and commitment to the Circle. Together, now, we will make ready for the final judgment."

"It would be a mistake for me to stay," he said.

"But not your first," she said, "and probably not your last. Lead us again! Where else are you needed more than here? Even a man with infinite lives has his limits."

She smiled, and he saw the girl he had met years ago, in another life. "The burden doesn't have to be yours alone anymore," she said. "But think of what we can pass down to the generations that follow."

The man relented and rejoined his people. And for a time, all that the woman had said seemed to come true. Many more followers flocked to Circle and their reputation and message spread all throughout Remnant. This was what he was here for, he thought. Perhaps, in the end, he would be able to rest.

And then everything changed.

Circle was invaded. Not by a group of Grimm this time, but by a group of warriors who stormed into the town and began attacking men, women, and children alike. The townspeople fought back valiantly, but the warriors were so strong that even with so many against so few, the Circle was losing. Many of them were injured before the man was summoned.

"Stop!" the man called. "What do you want here?"

A warrior stepped forward and grinned. She brandished a pair of large swords. "I came here to fight a god."

"I am just a man, and not even a very good one."

"That's not what I hear. Don't you use magic? Do you die and come back to life? That's a god."

The Infinite Man

"I can't help what you've heard about me." The man shot the woman a pointed look. "But in my experience, gods are far less than the stories told about them. I assure you, I am no god, and I don't want to fight you."

"You don't have a choice," the warrior said.

"We always have a choice. We can choose to help others instead of hurting them. We can choose how we want to live, and how we want to die." The man looked around at the people who had grown close to him. "But we also must accept the consequences of our choices."

"Here's your choice, then. Fight me, or we will kill everyone here."

"If I win, you will leave?" the man asked.

"The fight is to the death. If you win, my people will take my body and go," the warrior said.

"And if I lose?"

"We'll take *your* body and go."

"And you will leave my people alone?" the man asked. "You give your word?"

The warrior nodded.

"Very well. I accept," the man said.

"No!" the woman cried. "Don't do this."

The man took her hands. "If I die, it's just a minor inconvenience. If you die, our future dies with you."

The man turned away to face the warrior.

In a moment, the two of them were in combat. One of his opponent's blades was infused with purple Dust; each time her blade clashed against the man's staff, it unbalanced him for a moment. Her other sword used yellow Dust to send jolts of lightning through him when their weapons touched. If he tried to keep his distance, she fired powerful energy blasts at him, endangering not only him but all his people. And when she brought her weapons together, she was able to pull objects toward her. Thus, after a short while, she was able to disarm him.

The man had other powers, and he was able to deliver a number of blows against her even without his staff; but whether by Semblance or purple Dust, her feet always remained firmly rooted to the ground. No matter how hard he tried, he could not throw her or knock her down.

"You see," he said to his people, "any powerful Aura or Semblance can make someone appear godlike."

"I'm flattered, and impressed that you are teaching right up until the end," the warrior said, narrowing her eyes. "But I will still crush you."

She brought her swords together and the man became heavier. Each step he tried to take toward her was a battle.

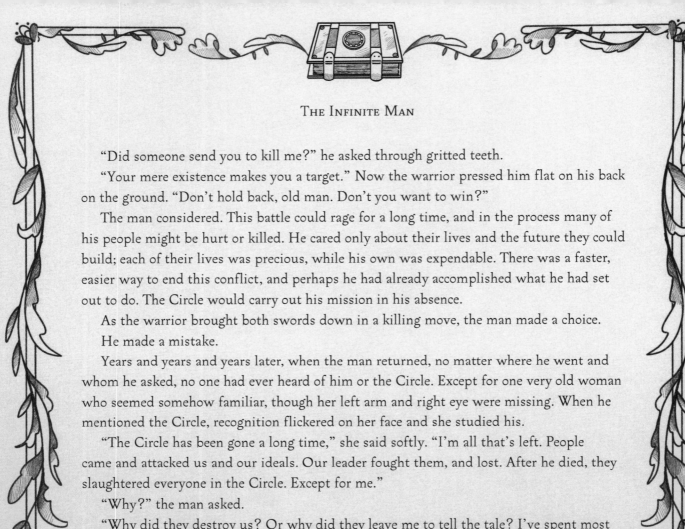

THE INFINITE MAN

"Did someone send you to kill me?" he asked through gritted teeth.

"Your mere existence makes you a target." Now the warrior pressed him flat on his back on the ground. "Don't hold back, old man. Don't you want to win?"

The man considered. This battle could rage for a long time, and in the process many of his people might be hurt or killed. He cared only about their lives and the future they could build; each of their lives was precious, while his own was expendable. There was a faster, easier way to end this conflict, and perhaps he had already accomplished what he had set out to do. The Circle would carry out his mission in his absence.

As the warrior brought both swords down in a killing move, the man made a choice.

He made a mistake.

Years and years and years later, when the man returned, no matter where he went and whom he asked, no one had ever heard of him or the Circle. Except for one very old woman who seemed somehow familiar, though her left arm and right eye were missing. When he mentioned the Circle, recognition flickered on her face and she studied his.

"The Circle has been gone a long time," she said softly. "I'm all that's left. People came and attacked us and our ideals. Our leader fought them, and lost. After he died, they slaughtered everyone in the Circle. Except for me."

"Why?" the man asked.

"Why did they destroy us? Or why did they leave me to tell the tale? I've spent most of my life turning that question over and over in my mind, and I believe the answer is the same: So that everyone would know the folly of placing their hopes and faith in one man." She looked away. "Not even a very good man."

The man knew that if she asked who he was, he would not be able to lie to her, as painful as the truth would be. But she didn't ask,
and that hurt even more.

Instead, she turned her back on him and hobbled away. And he let her go.

Many leaders have risen up through Remnant's history as false gods or by seizing control. And often people point to "The Infinite Man" as a cautionary tale of what can go wrong when you place too much faith or power in one person—or at least they point to some version of this story. Like the man who supposedly lived multiple lives, there are many variations of this tale, which in some cases are quite contradictory.

In fact, few stories have been told in so many different ways over the years, or lend themselves so easily to being used as propaganda pushing one agenda or another. In certain hands, the lesson here is about the danger of following "weak" leaders or those who seem too good to be true. Or it's about the risk of putting others before yourself. Or it's about being careful not to place unrealistic expectations on people. What does it mean to you?

This story reveals a different lesson for me whenever I read it, but in general I have a less cynical take: I think it's about the power of belief and how it can move people to action, for good or for ill or for a mixture of both. Trust is one of the most powerful forces in this world, and it is not to be abused or dismissed. As the story is related here, the "infinite man" placed his trust in the girl as much as she did in him, and perhaps they set their expectations too high on both sides. It's only natural for us to want or need to believe in something higher and bigger than ourselves. Some people still worship gods, while others insist that we must be our own salvation. But the world doesn't work in absolutes, so why can't it be both?

This rendition—in which the man indeed is everything he claims to be—is the most romantic and, I think, balanced version of the story, which I have cobbled together from a variety of differing accounts in an effort to paint a larger and clearer picture, one that is slightly more sympathetic to the man. He is alternately portrayed as a hero or a fool—and again I say, why can't it be both? Less commonly, he is represented as the villain. In response, I offer another interpretation for your consideration: Good intentions do not always have good results. We are all fallible. We all make mistakes. And forgiveness of those failures goes hand in hand with trust.

Although I have embellished this story slightly—attributing motives to the man's actions based on my own assumptions and, admittedly, my own prejudices and belief that there is good in all of us—no one who wasn't there could know what really happened. And even then, they would only have a small part of the story. Therefore, I leave it to you to decide whether this man is worthy of forgiveness.

Truth itself is not an absolute, and everyone is free to make their own choices.

The Two Brothers

RECORDED BY QROW BRANWEN

In the beginning, a dragon traveled the universe in search of other beings like himself. In all the realms and all the worlds, across every plane of existence, he found no one and nothing else. Finally, overcome with loneliness, the dragon decided to create a companion with whom he could share the cosmos and eternity—an equal, fashioned in his own image. Because even an all-powerful god cannot make something from nothing, the dragon divided himself and all his magic into two halves.

However, he destroyed himself in the act of creation. The old god was no more; in his place were two brothers, a dragon of pure light, and his shadow, a dragon of unfathomable darkness. They were new gods with shared memories and complementary abilities—and each thought that he was the original, and the other his copy. Though they had distinct personalities and competing desires, they were still connected and did not feel whole unless they were together. Since they could not agree on where to go, they decided to create a world for themselves. And as they were bored by the vast, lifeless universe, they decided to populate that world with other living beings to entertain them.

Whatever the God of Light created, the God of Darkness mimicked in his own way. The God of Light fashioned a sun, while his brother made a moon. The God of Light made a green continent covered in lush trees, grasses, plants, and flowers—the God of Darkness added barren deserts, rocky mountains, jagged crevasses in the earth. The God of Light breathed life into animals to explore the new world, while his brother birthed creatures of Grimm that were but their dark reflections.

One day the God of Light approached his brother. "I have been trying to create a beautiful world for us, but your creations spoil it."

"Your creations are almost as dull as the unending void was," said the God of Darkness. "If this place is going to entertain us, we need to make things lively." With that, the God of Darkness brought forth earthquakes and volcanoes that tore his brother's continent apart into smaller lands, boiled the oceans, rained fire and ash, and wiped out all the living things. "Look how they run!" The God of Darkness laughed. "Look how they die."

Troubled, the God of Light did what he could to repair the damage and rebuild the lost lives, but each time he did, the God of Darkness invented some new catastrophe to destroy them—and worse, make them suffer as they died. All while his dark nightmare beasts multiplied and spread across the world.

"Brother," said the God of Light one day. "Why do you take pleasure in torturing and destroying my creations?"

The God of Darkness smiled. "You take so much joy in their creation, I merely want you to be able to do more of it."

"But they are living things. They have feelings, and you are causing them pain."

"They do not reason as we do. They don't even know what they are. They have no understanding of their past, nor do they plan for their future. They are mere playthings for our amusement."

It had started out that way, but the God of Light had grown attached to all the different forms of life he had brought forth. In each of the animals he made, from the insects to the whales, he saw a small part of himself. Even gods cannot fashion something from nothing, and the brothers had given much of their essence to their creations. When his creations suffered, the God of Light felt some measure of their agony.

The God of Light wanted his brother to see the world as he did, to comprehend the responsibility that came with their immense power. And so, he made a bold proposal:

"What if we create a new form of life together, one more capable and fascinating than the animals and insects? We can make them aware of what they are, and empower them to control and shape their world."

The God of Darkness was intrigued. "If

they can think and communicate as we do, they won't be as predictable as the things you've made before."

"There is one condition, Brother," said the God of Light. "If we create these beings together, then we must share in any decisions about their fate. You must promise not to wipe them out on a whim; they must have the chance to find their own destiny and rule or ruin this world we have made for them."

The God of Darkness agreed, and they set to work.

Their joint creation required qualities that would set them apart from the animals and raise them closer to the gods themselves. With this goal in mind, each god prepared a gift for the new beings.

"I will give them knowledge of themselves and their world," said the God of Darkness. "So they can comprehend life and death, and thus they will also know fear."

The God of Light said, "And I will give them free will, the power to decide what to do with that knowledge and choose their own place in the world."

And thus Humanity was born. Because they embodied the essence of both brothers, Humans were capable of both creation and destruction, with the freedom and knowledge to choose their actions along a path of light or darkness.

For a time, the brothers were satisfied with what they had made together and they watched Humanity adapt and flourish. People spread across the planet, and if the God of Darkness occasionally tossed adversity their way in the form of natural disasters like a flood or tornado, the God of Light then blessed them with bountiful harvests and fair weather.

The God of Darkness was interested in testing the Humans' limits and admired their resourcefulness. Following a devastating earthquake, rather than give in to despair and accept failure, Humans rebuilt their homes— stronger than before, so they would survive the next quake. And though they grieved their lost loved ones, they picked up and pressed on. The God of Light underestimated the Humans, overprotective of their creations, but the God of Darkness saw how they thrived in facing challenges and grew in overcoming them.

But there was one danger that proved impossible for them to handle: the dark monstrosities the God of Darkness had unleashed, what Humanity called Creatures of Grimm.

The Grimm hated Humans, because of the light they saw inside them, and also because they were jealous; the God of Darkness had created the Grimm and forgotten them, but he was endlessly fascinated with Humans. The Grimm hunted Humanity to the ends of the world, and people

were all but defenseless against their sharp teeth and claws.

"Your abominations are killing the Humans," the God of Light told his brother. "Get rid of them."

"You protested whenever I wiped out your creations, but now you want to do the same to mine?" the God of Darkness snapped.

"Your creatures are not alive. They are crafted from malice and hate, with the sole purpose of destroying all that is good in the world."

The God of Darkness scowled. "Is that what you think of me, Brother? Never forget: You and I are the same."

Not exactly, the God of Light thought. "We share similar forms and powers, but we are quite different."

"I'm sorry I ever made you," they said at the same time.

Nevertheless, the God of Darkness refused to control or destroy his own creations. Secretly, he began making more Grimm to plague Humanity.

Also in secret, the God of Light granted Humanity a special gift to defend themselves against the Grimm. When the two brothers discovered what each had done, they argued. The argument became a battle that wreaked havoc across the world and sent many people into hiding. The desperate Humans prayed to their gods and asked if they were being punished. They asked for forgiveness. They begged for mercy.

Finally, the God of Light called a truce. "Look around, Brother. We are tearing the world apart."

"Let it burn," the God of Darkness said.

"We are making people miserable and interfering in Humanity's divine destiny," the God of Light said. "Perhaps it is time we leave the world in their hands and see what they make of it."

"Yes. Let us leave and go our separate ways at last," the God of Darkness agreed.

But just as the two brothers were so closely linked to each other, they were also closely tied to the world and their creations, most of all Humanity. In the act of creation, they had become less than they had been. They had given too much of themselves to be able to leave.

"We must take back our gifts," the God of Darkness said. "Reclaim our power and wipe

this experiment from existence."

"I disagree," the God of Light said. "And we promised to share in the fate of our joint creation." He gave a mighty yawn. "Let us rest, and when the time comes, we will see what Humanity has become in our absence. At that point, we will judge them. If they are worthy, we will take their forms and walk among them as equals. If not, we will take back our gifts and start over elsewhere. What do you say?"

"Who will decide whether they are worthy?" the God of Darkness said.

"Humanity will make it plain. If they come together in unity and find a way to destroy the evil in the world and within themselves, then they are worthy. If not . . . we will let them burn," the God of Light said.

"So shall it be." The two brothers agreed. But even in rest, they needed some distance from each other. Each dragon transformed himself into a new continent at one end of their world.

And there the dragons still sleep, until the day that the gods will waken, rise, and judge.

Ozpin's Notes

There are many versions of our creation story, but the Two Brothers figure in all of them. They appear in a variety of forms, but certain elements are always consistent: They arrived from a realm outside our own and together created the universe from nothing. And then they left us on our own.

Whether or not you believe in the Brothers, or in this story in particular, the underlying message still holds value: We are burdened with responsibility for our world, and we share a common destiny. Like the twin gods, we are intricately connected with one another, and if we can learn to work and live together, we can create things greater than the sum of their parts.

Remnant survived the Great War, but while the four kingdoms now cooperate and coexist, our bond seems tenuous. We have a fragile peace, and in some ways, we are more divided than ever. Even if the gods aren't real, even if they don't return to judge us for our deeds, we should act each day as though they are arriving tomorrow. In the end, we will be the arbiters of our fates. We will either create a beautiful, peaceful world and live in harmony together or destroy ourselves and our planet, and the gods will judge what we have chosen.

And if that seems too heavy a topic for a children's fable, at least there are dragons.

The Story of the Seasons

SOURCE: TRADITIONAL

eep in the forests of Remnant, beside a great and powerful river, there lived an old wizard. Blessed with magic but cursed with a long, lonely life, the wizard closed himself to everyone and everything in the world. So cold was his heart that the lands around him were covered in snow, the trees were bare, and animals and Creatures of Grimm alike avoided him. For centuries, no one disturbed his peace, if you can call it that, until he became more hermit than wizard. Then one day an unlikely visitor appeared outside his window. It was a young maiden, dressed in blue and white, sitting at the base of a tree. He didn't know where she had come from, and he assumed she was frozen, but when he called out to her from his window, she opened her eyes.

"You there! Are you all right?" he asked.

His voice cracked from age and disuse.

"I am fine, thank you for asking." She closed her eyes again.

"What are you doing here in the middle of nowhere?" he asked.

"This is not nowhere, since we are both here. I am doing the same as you. Pausing to take a rest before resuming a long journey."

The old wizard frowned. Finally, he opened his door and beckoned her inside. "Well, you should come inside before you freeze to death."

She rose and entered the hermit's home, which was not much warmer inside than outside. But she still thanked him.

"Who are you?" he asked. "Where did you come from?"

"My name is Winter, and where we came from is not as important as where we are going."

The wizard could not remember the last

time he had eaten, but he prepared a fire and cooked a simple meal for his unexpected guest, realizing that he, too, was hungry. They sipped plain soup from wooden bowls in silence, and when they were done, he asked her, "Do you know me? What do you know of my journey?"

"I do not know you, sir, but life is a journey for all of us, with a beginning, a middle, and an end."

"You seem quite wise for your years," he said.

"I have always been perceptive. I find that meditation helps clear the mind and improves focus when I lose my way. May I show you?"

The hermit nodded. Together they sat on the floor and Winter guided him in mental discipline. They meditated together every day, and at the end of several months, the old man had achieved the serenity and clarity of purpose that had eluded him for hundreds of years. His friendship with Winter ended his self-imposed solitude and warmed his heart; in turn, the frozen forest began to thaw around them.

One day, the hermit was astounded to hear a beautiful voice singing outside his house. He looked out his window and saw another young maiden, dressed in green, kneeling on the ground and digging in the dirt with her hands. She took seeds from a pouch tied around her slim waist and pushed them into the soft earth.

"Who's there?" he called. "What are you doing?"

Winter opened the door. "Oh! My sister is here!"

The two women hugged, while the old wizard watched in confusion.

"I am Spring," the newcomer said in a lyrical voice. "I am resting on a long journey. I find it's important to stop and smell the roses now and then, don't you?" A rosebush sprouted from her feet and blossomed at once with beautiful red roses.

"How did you do that?" the wizard asked.

"I have always been good at making things grow," Spring said.

"You say you are resting, but planting is hard work," he said.

"I find it relaxing, and hard work can be its own reward. Let me show you?"

The hermit hesitated, but then he relented. Together they planted a garden all around his house and every day they tended it. They gathered the fruits and vegetables that grew at an extraordinary rate, and their meals greatly

improved due to the fresh food and the lively company. Gradually life returned to the tired hermit and the forest, which flourished and became green and lush.

One day, the hermit heard laughter from outside. Before he had even rushed to the window, Winter and Spring said in harmony, "Our sister!"

They opened the door and ran outside, and soon the hermit heard the three of them laughing together. The third young maiden was clad in purple.

"Welcome," the hermit called from his window. "Please, tell me your name."

"My name is Summer," she said. "I am resting on a long journey."

Of course, thought the wizard. Aloud he said, "Why were you laughing? What's so funny?"

The woman looked at him with a bright smile on her face.

"Me?" he said incredulously. "I'll have you know I am a skilled wizard. No one has ever laughed at me in my life."

"Perhaps not to your face," she replied. "Or perhaps because no one was here to see the folly in a great man who can do so much yet does nothing."

The hermit felt a surge of anger, but his training with Winter had shown him how to recognize the truth in things. In his heart, he knew that Summer was right.

"Your ridicule is justified," he admitted.

Summer changed the subject. "It seems silly to be cooped up inside on such a beautiful, warm day," she said. "Why limit yourself to observing the world through a small window when you can walk through that door and be a part of it?" Joyfully, Summer twirled around.

Now that she mentioned it, the wizard did find that his house had grown stuffy. He stepped outside and took a deep breath. The fresh air and the warmth of the sun filled him with such energy and life that he felt rejuvenated. It was so pleasant outdoors that he had no desire to withdraw inside his home, his self-imposed prison for all these years. For the next several months, the wizard and the three maidens spent every waking moment outside and slept under the stars. It had been many lifetimes since he had felt such a strong connection to other people and the world.

One day, as they settled down to an outdoor feast on a balmy evening, the wizard felt a sudden chill. He noticed a delicate young woman standing under an apple tree. He watched with bemusement as Winter, Spring, and Summer ran toward her, joining hands and dancing around the tree. Her features were similar to those of her sisters, but she was wearing orange.

The wizard stayed by the table until the women beckoned him to join them. Before he could ask, the new arrival introduced herself.

"My name is Fall. I am resting on a long journey. Who are you?"

"Me?" the wizard said. "I am but an old hermit—"

"Hermits do not invite people into their home or share their food," Fall pointed out. "Hermits don't celebrate all summer long."

"That is a fair point. However, I have lived in these woods alone for a long time, with no one to love and nothing to my name. Your sisters have brought me new life."

Fall opened her arms wide. "But sir, do you not see? You have so much already."

As the four maidens and the wizard enjoyed a meal together, he realized that Fall was right. Somehow, the sisters had restored to him all that he had lost, and given him much more than he ever could have dreamed of. They spent several more months in one another's company, but the wizard knew that their time together was running out. The days grew shorter and cooler, until one day, the maidens announced that it was time for them to continue their journeys.

"Journeys? Are you not traveling together?" the wizard asked. He didn't dare voice the hope he had hidden in his heart: that they would decide to stay with him, or invite him to join them as they ventured out into the world.

"Our paths lead us in different directions," Winter said. "To the four corners of Remnant. But we are grateful to you for providing us with a much-needed break and hospitality."

"Why me?" he asked. "Why did the four of you come here and open my eyes? To share with me your gifts? What makes me so special?"

The sisters looked at one another, perplexed. Finally, Fall spoke.

"We did not choose you in particular. We wander everywhere and do what we can for everyone, because we are able."

The old wizard was at a loss. Never in his many years had he come across such kindness. He decided that he had to repay them with a gift of his own.

"I have incredible magic, and if you will allow me, I would like to share a portion of it with each of you," he said.

"That is too generous," Summer said. "We cannot take your magic."

"As you once pointed out, I have not been doing much with it. If you accept my gift, the four of you, who already do so much, can accomplish even more good in the world."

The sisters discussed it quietly among themselves before they ultimately accepted the wizard's offer. He summoned as much of his

magic as he could and bestowed it upon four maidens.

"I grant you magic of your own, mastery over the elements, the very powers of nature. May you use it to aid others just as you have aided me."

The wizard was exhausted, but he felt lighter and more optimistic about the future than he had in a long time. With the four maidens sharing his magic, knowing they would be out there working for the good of all, he no longer felt so alone.

"Thank you," they said. "We will do our best. Now what will you do?"

The wizard looked back at his house. "My rest is over. It is time for me to resume my journey and work as well."

One by one, the sisters left. Before they did, they made one final promise: to return each and every year, to visit their dear friend.

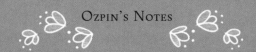

Ozpin's Notes

As with many fables, "The Story of the Seasons" was first told in order to explain natural phenomena that people observed in the world such as the sun, the moon, and the Creatures of Grimm. In this case, the seasons—winter, spring, summer, and fall—are personified as maidens who wield elemental powers.

Things that we cannot understand traditionally have been attributed to magic, which anyone from Atlas will tell you is virtually indistinguishable from advanced technology or, in this case, the science of weather. Of course magic isn't only a fairy tale—it really does exist in our world, through the expert application of Dust. No wonder that so many stories concern magic and magic users, and imagine another time and place in which magic was even more plentiful and potent.

However, despite the prevalence of powerful wizards and witches in our fairy tales, the world has never known the levels of magic described here—for which we should be grateful. I fear that if unrestricted magic use were possible, the results would be chaotic and catastrophic. Better to leave such fanciful notions comfortably in the realm of fantasy!

It is also worth noting that the true powers of the four maidens in this story had nothing to do with magic and everything to do with who they are. The maidens' natural gifts, which they shared with the old hermit before he imbued them with his own magic, are clear representations of the close interplay between strong Aura and Semblances. And the lessons he learned are broadly applicable to each of us: Learn to center yourself and think reflectively to gain awareness of who you are and what you can contribute to the world. Try to nurture the life around you and remember to 'stop and smell the roses.' Don't view the world at a distance—take an active part in it and the events around you. And finally, be thankful for what you have and show your gratitude.

The Girl in the Tower

SOURCE: ANONYMOUS

I also urge everyone to consider this story's moral and take it to heart as I have: Do what you can for others, because you are able.

A long, long time ago, in a faraway land, there lived a cruel lord and his beautiful daughter.

The lord had once been a good man, blessed by the gods with strength, bravery, charm, and powerful magic. In his youth he had traveled Remnant in search of adventure, fame, fortune, and love. He saved many people, slew many monstrous beasts, and brought many wicked men to justice. When he rescued a princess from a brutish gang of kidnappers, he gained everything he had ever desired: a wife, a castle and land, and recognition across the kingdom as a mighty hero. What more could a man want?

Just one thing: a son and heir. When his wife became pregnant, the whole castle rejoiced. But soon the lord's fortune reversed. His beloved fell ill, gave birth to a baby girl, and lost her own life in the process. The lord locked his daughter in the highest tower of the castle and retreated to his chambers to grieve. Only he and the girl's nanny were allowed in or out of her tower room, on punishment of death.

Many weeks passed before the lord visited his baby girl for the first time, and he refused to hold her no matter how much the nanny encouraged or even begged him to. Over the years, his daily visits grew shorter. Then they became visits two or three times a week. By his daughter's eleventh birthday, he was visiting only once a week.

"Why must I stay in this tower?" the girl would ask him.

"I am protecting you from anything or anyone that might harm you. You are the most precious thing in the world to me. I could not bear to lose you."

He brought her food and presents: dresses and hairpins, brushes and dolls, but nothing that she could use against him or to take her own life. The single, tall window was enchanted so she could see out but not extend even a hand over the sill, and she assumed no one could enter the room through it either. However, when she attempted to toss out her father's gifts she discovered something interesting: Inanimate objects could pass through the magical barrier.

Since the girl could not leave the tower, her nanny brought the outside world to her: She taught the girl to read and stole books for her from the castle library. The girl lived hundreds of lives through other people's stories, and she harbored the impossible dream of venturing beyond the tower one day, finding true love, and becoming a kind and generous queen with her own castle and daughters.

Meanwhile, miserable and alone, the lord's sorrow gradually twisted into resentment. He raged against the unfairness of the gods and took out his anger on his staff. He became obsessed with increasing his wealth,

as if money could replace the love of his life, increasing land taxes on his tenants and cutting his staff's wages. Paranoid about losing all he cherished, he dismissed half of his servants and replaced them with trained soldiers to protect his riches and defend his castle.

By the girl's sixteenth birthday, the king was visiting only once a month, whenever the whole moon was visible from her tower window.

"This was your mother's favorite place in the castle," he told the girl. "She loved gazing out that window."

"And now it is my prison," the girl said.

"You aren't my prisoner. You're my daughter."

"Then let me go," she begged.

"I cannot. Someone would abduct you and demand a ransom," the lord said. "Or worse."

But the girl realized that the lord did not love her as a parent loves a child. Rather, he thought of her as just one of his treasures, to be jealously hoarded like his gold and jewels. She decided she had to escape, and she desired to punish her father for his cruelty.

She was not strong enough to fight her way out of the tower, but she was smart. She struck upon a plan.

"Thank you for the beautiful necklaces and

rings, Father," she told him. "You give me everything I could ever want, except . . ."

"What is it?" the knight asked. "What else would make you happy, my dear?"

Freedom, she thought. But she bit back the word, for that kind of talk made him angry and violent.

"Pens and paper," she said. "I love reading, and I would like to try writing stories of my own."

He saw no harm in her request and brought her pens and paper.

"Perhaps when I visit you will read your stories to me," the lord said.

The girl used the materials he gave her to record her own story, with an open ending: a promise

that who ever defeated the lord and freed her from the tower would inherit the castle and

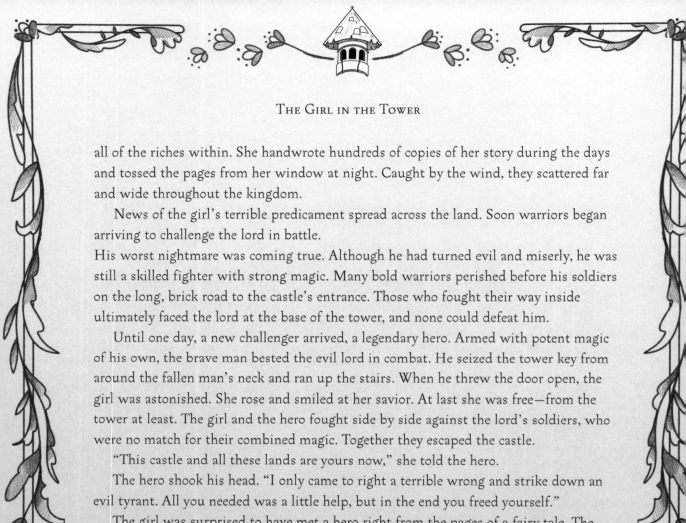

all of the riches within. She handwrote hundreds of copies of her story during the days and tossed the pages from her window at night. Caught by the wind, they scattered far and wide throughout the kingdom.

News of the girl's terrible predicament spread across the land. Soon warriors began arriving to challenge the lord in battle.

His worst nightmare was coming true. Although he had turned evil and miserly, he was still a skilled fighter with strong magic. Many bold warriors perished before his soldiers on the long, brick road to the castle's entrance. Those who fought their way inside ultimately faced the lord at the base of the tower, and none could defeat him.

Until one day, a new challenger arrived, a legendary hero. Armed with potent magic of his own, the brave man bested the evil lord in combat. He seized the tower key from around the fallen man's neck and ran up the stairs. When he threw the door open, the girl was astonished. She rose and smiled at her savior. At last she was free—from the tower at least. The girl and the hero fought side by side against the lord's soldiers, who were no match for their combined magic. Together they escaped the castle.

"This castle and all these lands are yours now," she told the hero.

The hero shook his head. "I only came to right a terrible wrong and strike down an evil tyrant. All you needed was a little help, but in the end you freed yourself."

The girl was surprised to have met a hero right from the pages of a fairy tale. The hero was surprised to meet a smart and powerful girl who shared his curiosity about the world and a strong sense of justice. Neither was eager to go their separate ways.

"So, where should we go now?" the girl asked.

The hero offered her his hand. "Wherever you'd like."

The two fell deeply in love, planned adventures around the world, and lived happily ever after.

OZPIN'S NOTES

"The Girl in the Tower" is unique among fairy tales in that it is the only one in which the protagonist is credited with penning their own story; the girl essentially writes herself out of danger. It is steeped in an awareness of the nature of fairy tales and, in a sense, its own status as one of them. As a metafiction, this tale more than any other in this collection demonstrates the power of stories to create reality and shape our destinies, and the subtle influence storytellers have over their audiences.

This is how propaganda works, of course. Arguably, every fable was originally told for a purpose, either overt or hidden. Some were designed to communicate a moral lesson or instruct children on how to behave, while others were meant as warnings or to persuade people into believing a certain thing. The girl in the tower shared a version of her story intended to elicit sympathy and motivate people to come to her aid—but in the process she also doomed many warriors to die in the attempt. Her story did not include the whole truth, and how much of it might have been false? One must always be prepared to think about and question everything they read or hear, especially if they are told that it is absolute truth.

To me, this tale is also a reminder that the familiar stories we know are just small parts of a larger one—other moments come before "once upon a time" and still more follow "happily ever after." It is the storyteller who decides where a tale begins and when it ends, and if you look far enough ahead, even a story with a happy ending may reveal itself as a tragedy, and heroes may turn out to be villains.

Hopefully, the reverse is also true.

The Gift of the Moon

SOURCE: TRADITIONAL

In a very distant past, much longer ago than anyone can remember, people wondered why nights were so dark. In those days, there was only the sun to illuminate the whole world, going around and around the sky. But the sun could only do so much, and half of the time, half of the world was brightly lit while the other half was cast into darkness.

"We could accomplish a lot more each day if only we had light all the time," the people reasoned. "We would not have to sleep at night or fear monsters in the shadows." They set their minds to finding a solution.

At first, they tried to slow the sun down on its travels by distracting it with a steady stream of compliments. For a while the sun crawled across the sky more slowly as it listened to their praise. But then someone said, "We can always count on you rising each morning and setting each evening at the same time!" His friends shushed him, but the sun had already heard it and realized it was far behind schedule. It hurried on its way. By the next morning, the sun was back on course, drooping lower and shining more dimly than usual.

Then the people pointed out that the sun worked so hard, with long hours day after day. Didn't it deserve a little rest? "Why not stay in one place for a while instead of constantly going around and around the world?" they suggested. The sun liked the sound of a break, so it fixed itself in place for a while. While the land below it enjoyed an unending day,

everywhere else it was night. Where the sun lingered, it grew sweltering. Crops died, and no one could get any sleep. In the darker parts of the land, it was cold. These crops died, too, while people huddled under blankets to stay warm and often fell asleep.

In both places, the people resolved to try something else.

"Perhaps if you moved a little faster," the people said. Well rested from its vacation, the sun was agreeable to the idea. It zoomed across the sky faster than it ever had before. "Faster," the people cried. "Faster!

The sun moved faster. It moved so fast it was a bright line streaking across the sky, and everywhere it was daylight. But only for a short while. This effort tired the sun out so much, it quickly burned out and crashed to the earth.

Oh no, the people thought as unending night settled over the world. *We broke it!*

Realizing that they should have left well enough alone, they went in search of the fallen sun. They found it in a large, smoldering valley that had not been there before. Or they found most of it; a large chunk of the sun had shattered and now the pieces lay all over the land. Everyone helped gather the remnants and piece the sun back together. When they had put it together as best they could, they hoisted the sun back up into the sky. But the sun was now a weak shadow of its former self, and its shattered fragments kept drifting off to float nearby. Its pale glow barely illuminated the night and brought no warmth at all.

"What's wrong?" they cried. "Why is your light so dim?"

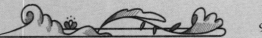

The sun explained that when it had broken, much of its light had spilled on the ground below. It could barely hold on to the little that was left, which was slowly leaking out and scattering through the night sky as stars. The people panicked and grieved and pitied themselves. But they were persistent and they were clever. They decided they would have to build a replacement sun, and if they were going to make one, it should be even better and brighter than before.

Everyone in the world came together for this massive undertaking. The people gathered all their resources and fashioned a glass orb even larger than the original. They collected all the sun's spilled light and poured it into the orb, which glowed brighter and hotter. Before everyone and everything around it burned up, they hoisted the sun into the heavens. They fastened one end of a rope around the old sun and the other end around the new sun on the other side of the world, so as the one moved it towed the other along behind.

When the new sun was overhead, it was daylight, and when the shattered sun traveled across the sky, it cast a gentler light that allowed people to sleep or work however they pleased.

"We should have thought of this sooner," the people said.

The only one unhappy with this arrangement was the broken sun, which was never as bright as it was before and now had to do twice the work.

"You're much prettier this way," the people said. "We could never look at you properly before because you were too bright."

The Gift of the Moon

"Even though I'm broken?" the sun said.

"It gives you character," they insisted. "Besides, now your light has spread all over and made the night sky beautiful."

"That's true."

"Don't worry. We'll always know that other sun is a fake," they promised.

But despite the people's compliments and reassurances, the broken sun never stopped mooning over its golden days, when it was alone in the sky and the world had basked in its warmth. And that's why we call it the moon today.

"You can't put the moon back together" is a well-known phrase that usually means something broken cannot be fixed. However, its original meaning, as traced back to this age-old fable, is this: If something cannot be fixed, you should start over.

One interpretation of this story focuses on the fact that the people caused the problem in the first place. But in my view, it is only natural for us to want to bring more light into the world and "reach for the sun." And on the brighter side, if you'll excuse the pun, people were also part of the solution. They not only replaced the sun, a celestial gift from the all-powerful God of Light, but also improved upon it through their own ingenuity. Most importantly, they could not have accomplished this magnificent, godly feat without uniting for a common purpose in a way they never had before.

The world once was divided between day and night, light and darkness, but by coming together, and overcoming their inherent jealousy and resentment, people made the darkness just a little bit brighter for all.

Ozpin's Afterword

And now we find ourselves, here at the end.

All things come to an end, at least for a time, and this collection is no different. But take heart, dear reader, for life is an ongoing process of renewal, and endings simply make way for fresh beginnings. When you finish a story, turn the page and start a new one. When you close a book, pick up another. Or of course you may always read this one again.

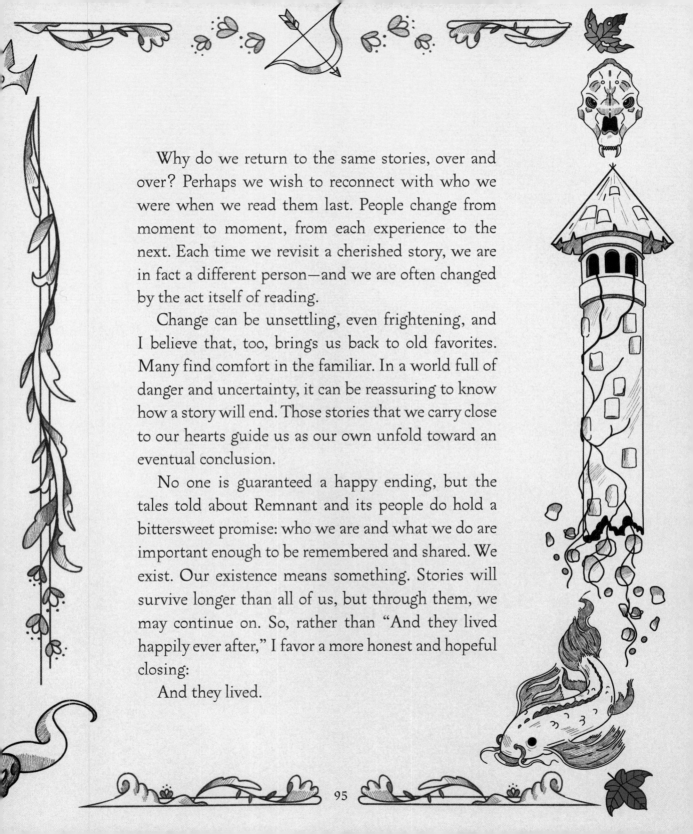

Why do we return to the same stories, over and over? Perhaps we wish to reconnect with who we were when we read them last. People change from moment to moment, from each experience to the next. Each time we revisit a cherished story, we are in fact a different person—and we are often changed by the act itself of reading.

Change can be unsettling, even frightening, and I believe that, too, brings us back to old favorites. Many find comfort in the familiar. In a world full of danger and uncertainty, it can be reassuring to know how a story will end. Those stories that we carry close to our hearts guide us as our own unfold toward an eventual conclusion.

No one is guaranteed a happy ending, but the tales told about Remnant and its people do hold a bittersweet promise: who we are and what we do are important enough to be remembered and shared. We exist. Our existence means something. Stories will survive longer than all of us, but through them, we may continue on. So, rather than "And they lived happily ever after," I favor a more honest and hopeful closing:

And they lived.

About the Author

Photo © Ellen B. Wright

E. C. MYERS was assembled in the U.S. from Korean and German parts and raised by a single mother and the public library in Yonkers, New York. He is the author of numerous short stories and four young adult books: the Andre Norton Award – winning *Fair Coin*, *Quantum Coin*, *The Silence of Six*, and *Against All Silence*. E. C. currently lives with his wife, son, and three doofy pets in Pennsylvania. You can find traces of him all over the Internet, but especially at ecmyers.net and on Twitter @ecmyers.